Praise for *Criterium*

"Jones' prose in *Criterium* is like a shot of adrenaline to the heart. Once you turn that first page, you give over any control you once had, and this book will steamroll you into the ride of your life...you can almost feel the wind in your face and the heat on your flesh...he writes this story to within an inch of its life... there are moments of frenzied paranoia and then subtle and melancholic moments of sadness, grief and aloneness. It's intoxicating."
—**Ross Jeffery, Bram Stoker nominated author of** *Juniper* **and** *Tome*

"What a ride. *Criterium* is unpredictable, fast-paced, and bleeds with heart. Tyler Jones is one to watch."
—**Scott J. Moses, author of** *Hunger Pangs*

"A haunting masterclass in storytelling."
—**Eric LaRocca, author of** *Things Have Gotten Worse Since We Last Spoke*

"*Criterium* is a high-octane ride in every way imaginable. A magnificent example of the type of storytelling that can be achieved through the novella form...mixes relatable real-life grief with metaphor that embodies what addiction horror can be."
—**Brennan LaFaro, author of** *Slattery Falls*

"*Criterium* is a gut-wrenching emotional rollercoaster into the real-life horrors of addiction and sorrow. Tyler Jones knows how to hit you where it'll hurt. I highly recommend this story to readers of the supernatural horror genre that are looking for a story that will leave you numb and breathless."
—Andrew Fowlow, *The Horror Oasis*

"Jones managed to write one of my favorite books of the year and I don't say that lightly. His prose is flawless, the ambiance is stunning, and the story has a beautiful darkness...it consumed me in a big way. It will eat you up and spit you out. *Criterium* is intelligent, haunting, and emotional with a compelling plot that combines the hell of addiction with horror seamlessly. I couldn't put it down if I wanted."
—Janelle Janson, *SheReadsWithCats*

"Tyler Jones' first novella is an unflinching and compassionate view into the black hole of addiction and grief. An intriguing and novel premise that drags real life horror into the depths of the supernatural—compulsively readable."
—Laurel Hightower, author of *Crossroads* and *Whispers in the Dark*

By Tyler Jones

Almost Ruth
Enter Softly
The Dark Side of the Room
Criterium

TYLER JONES

**DARK ROOM
PRESS**

Copyright © Tyler Jones, 2021

Cover art by David Mack
www.davidmack.net

Interior title illustrations by Ryan Mills
rtm.art.inq@gmail.com

Cover design and interior layout by Scott Cole
www.13visions.com

For more information about the author, visit
www.tylerjones.net

For Quinn, ride fast

Cycles

An Introduction to Criterium
By Jeremy Robert Johnson

If the stats are to be believed, some kind of modern day demon is haunting your family right now. Doesn't matter who you are, where you live, what you believe— someone in your family is in the throes of possession right now, and they're struggling. Might be somebody you love. Might be somebody you can barely love anymore, because these demons do hard things to a person, and to anyone in their vicinity. Hell, it might even be you struggling.

Thing is, these demons—alcoholism, drug addiction, depression, intrusive thoughts, eating disorders—they don't shake off so easy. Shouting "The power of Christ compels you!" and flinging a couple bottles of holy water won't unseat these beasts once they've got their claws in deep. No, you're looking at a much longer road. Harder work. DT's, backsliding, meds of varying effect, apologies, psychotherapy, reconnection, regret, painful honesty. Figuring out what it takes to suffer less. It's full-on spiritual/physical/psychological warfare, and the part that a lot of folks don't want to own up to is that it never ends.

Worse, even if you don't let these things take you to the grave, even if you fight to get free, they might just hop out of you and take up residence in someone you love. They'll haunt you in a brand new way. These possessions can be a real family affair, and sometimes that hurts even more.

Tyler Jones gets this. The slim and relentlessly propulsive novella you're holding now wants to tell you a story about these hauntings. *Criterium* is a deeply-felt story about addiction, and hurt, and that struggle to break free, but it's also a story of possessions, immolations, and strange figures moving behind the windows of a very dangerous house on Archer Way. This is a broken-hearted ballad about a boy named Zach Ayers, haunted not only by the memory of his beleaguered father, but by the malevolent forces which find Zach a perfectly suitable substitute for his old man. This is small-town Bradbury with a world-weary mean streak: even the magic here seems perfectly happy to break your bones and drag your face across asphalt. And in careful concert with all the supernatural sleight-of-hand, this is, quite crucially, a book which understands what it feels like to hear your mother cry from the next room— how deep that pain is, how much it eats away at you—and the quicksand of knowing that the thing that caused her that pain is, well…it's you. In being haunted, you begin to haunt the ones you love, and the suffering inherent in that is a black hole all its own. At one point Zach Ayers reflects on the aspirations he had as a child, and then he thinks, *"Now look at you."* That's a moment and a mirror that I feel we can all understand, and another example of how *Criterium* roots us in empathy and universal experience before it races off into the weird unknown of its elegant allegories.

Not to say that this story is all Sturm und Drang— there are darkly humorous moments, a fascinatingly eclectic drug dealer (who deserves his own damn book, assuming Hazard escaped this one alive), and though the book's emotional core may be broken-hearted it still beats. It still radiates a sense of love.

So maybe you're like me, and addiction doesn't just run in your family, it gallops. Or maybe you've personally met one or more of those demons listed above, and you're still in the fight. Or maybe you're one of the statistically lucky few, and you haven't experienced the type of haunting that drives this book. Regardless, I believe this is a story you'll feel in your bones.

And you may have noticed that I've said a lot more about how this book feels, and what it's about, than *how* it tells its story. That's because Tyler Jones' *Criterium*, truly, is a trip, and there are strange surprises inside, humming, vibrating, just waiting for you to take this ride. So turn the page, hold on tight, and if you're lucky I'll see you on the other side...

cri•te•ri•um

/ˌkrīˈtirēəm/

(noun)

a one-day bicycle race on a circuit road course.

Flicker, Fade

Their voices came through the walls, hushed at first, just hoarse whispers. But they grew louder, more agitated, the longer they spoke. Zach Ayers lay awake in bed, listening. He'd much rather have his headphones on, music drowning out all the noise in his head, but he'd learned long ago how important it was to know what the fights were about. For example, two months earlier he'd found out Mom was taking him and his little sister, Tessa, to visit their aunt in Washington. He'd fallen asleep knowing they were running from Dad, even if just for a few days, to scare him into becoming someone Zach was no longer sure he had the ability to be.

Dad had missed Zach's basketball game tonight, which he'd promised to be at, so Zach didn't expect him to be home for the late dinner. The way Mom stabbed her fork into the green beans on her plate—scraping against the porcelain with an awful sound—Zach knew the fight was going to be a bad one. They all sat around the table—well, all of them except Dad—eating in silence. But Mom's silence had a certain sound to it, a sort of psychic ringing and rush of exhaled breath.

There was a place set for Dad, but it wasn't a plate and fork. Instead, it was a small stack of paper and torn-open envelopes. Paper that had been accordion folded and wouldn't lay flat.

Zach saw a red word on the top of one page: OVERDUE.

If he could hear Mom and Dad fighting, Tessa definitely could. Her room was closer.

Zach had been asleep until Dad came home, opening and closing the door loud, like he had no idea it was nearly one o'clock in the morning. They'd been fighting ever since.

Zach glanced at the red, glowing numbers of his clock—it was close to two a.m. now—got up, opened his door, and went out into the hall. The voices were even louder, and Dad's had that lazy growl, like he was forcing the words out through a mouth that didn't want them to escape. Zach tiptoed down the hall to his sister's room and went inside. He waited a second for his eyes to adjust to the nightlight plugged into the wall. The voices were louder in her room, clearer. He went over to the bed, and his heart broke a little when he saw Tessa, lying on her stomach with a pillow over her head. Both hands clamping it over her ears.

She jerked when Zach touched her shoulder, made a little squeak, and rolled over, her eyes open wide. Zach wrapped his arms around her and pulled her close.

"They'll stop soon," he whispered.

Tessa sniffed. "This one's worse," she said. "Dad spent all the money he made. We don't have enough for the rent."

"Shit," Zach said, then quickly added, "sorry."

He rubbed her back with one hand, felt her muscles slowly relax.

"What did Mom say?" he asked.

Tessa sat back, wiped her snotty nose on her pajama sleeve.

"There isn't enough to get him to rehab, so she said he'd have to be strong and do it himself."

Zach's heart slipped down into his stomach. He knew Dad couldn't do it. There was no way. Zach only had faint memories of their father before the drugs, memories he clung to on nights like this. But the person Dad was now didn't have the strength, or the self-control, to stop something like this. Mom might as well tell him to go stand in front of a train and hold out his hand.

Sometimes Zach had trouble remembering who Dad was before the drugs. It was like there were two separate people in his memory that inhabited the same body. Every once in a while a memory would flicker into existence, a moment from when he was a kid and Dad was himself. The real him. Flicker, then fade.

Flicker, fade.

"If he missed your game he's probably going to miss the science fair too, won't he?" Tessa said, her face blank, eyes staring at the nightlight.

Zach had to bury to his own anger at Dad's absence. There was only one thing in the world that meant anything to Zach, and that was basketball. He wasn't great, but he was good. A starter on the JV team. And if he traced his love of the game back to its origin, it was being a kid and sitting with Dad on the couch, watching the Lakers on a lazy Sunday. It never even occurred to Zach at the time that Dad was asleep on the couch half the time, blissfully floating beneath the surface of the real world.

He makes promises he can't keep. No, Zach thought, won't keep. He won't even try.

"No," Zach whispered, smiling. "I'll bet he'll be there."

Tessa snorted, but her blank expression never changed.

"I'll talk to him about it," Zach said. "Remind him, you know."

The problem with Mom and Dad fighting, Zach knew, was that Mom's anger always made Dad feel even worse, so then off he'd go again, in search of something to erase whatever he felt. Guilt, fear, shame, regret… whatever it was, it would be gone by the time he came home again. Zach knew Mom slept on the floor of their room sometimes, just because she couldn't stand to share a bed with her husband.

The voices, mostly Mom now, reached a higher pitch than before and then collapsed into ragged weeping. God, how he hated to hear her like that.

"Lay down," he told Tessa. And when she did, he handed her the pillow. "Put this over your head and sing a song."

"Which song?" she asked.

"Doesn't matter. Whichever one is your favorite."

She did as he said, and he rubbed her back some more.

The term "heartbreak" was something his classmates said all time whenever they broke up with girlfriend or boyfriend. For the longest time he had no idea that the worst pain, the ache he felt now, came from hurting for your own flesh and blood.

Mom and Dad's bedroom door opened, slammed closed, and heavy footsteps pounded down the hall. Zach got up, inched Tessa's door open, and poked his head out. Mom was still crying, probably would be for a while, so he crept down the hall to the kitchen just as the front door was opening.

Zach didn't know what to say to make his dad stop from going outside, so he said the first thing that came to mind. "Tessa's scared," he said. "She needs you to tell her everything's okay."

Dad stopped in the open doorway, one hand still on the knob. His already slouched shoulders fell farther as he sighed.

Dad stayed facing the front yard. He wouldn't turn around, look at Zach.

"I'm sorry, son," Dad said. "Some things just don't change. We are what we are."

Zach almost said it out loud, but the words, even in his head, sounded too childlike.

Don't go. Dad, please don't go.

Because he knew exactly where Dad would go once he left. The gray house. Zach knew about it—everyone knew about it. How it remained occupied, operational, was anyone's guess, but Zach had seen enough zombies shuffling down Archer Way to know there was something in the house people wanted, something that shut down everything that made them who they were.

Dad sighed again, then he stepped out into the cold and shut the door behind him.

Zach stood in the kitchen, alone, the sound of Mom's hopeless crying echoing down the hall. He watched Dad from the

22

window, trudging through the snow-covered lawn, leaving a trail of black footprints. He wore just a blue flannel shirt, no jacket, and Zach wondered if he could even feel the cold.

Zach thought maybe he could run after him and catch up, and maybe the sight of his son would be enough for Dad to come back home and sweat out the chemicals. So Zach stopped by his room just long enough to grab a sweatshirt, then he ran outside—but the street was quiet and dark, and his dad was already gone.

1

A screaming tore across the night and echoed down the street of the residential neighborhood. The voice, hoarse and afraid, was male. Adult by the sound of it, filled with pain. It charged down Archer Way, moving past one house after the other in rapid succession.

A landscaper, in bed with his wife, jerked awake when he heard the sound. He rolled over and looked at the glowing red numbers of the clock. The scream rose and fell in volume, like a siren. *Probably joyriders,* the landscaper thought. *Drunk kids out for a drive.* He rolled back over and covered his head with a pillow.

A few houses down, a realtor lay wide awake staring at the ceiling. She hadn't sold a house since before Thanksgiving, and the money in her bank account wouldn't be enough to pay the mortgage next month. She'd managed to keep away from the online poker for the last few weeks, but her fingers itched to touch the screen of her phone, play the cards. She sat up when she heard something like an animal howling. It stopped, then started again, this time closer.

The sound echoed again, right outside her window. The skin on the realtor's arms rose in tiny bumps. She jumped up and opened the curtains just as the sound passed by. A blur of light moved down the street and took the howl with it.

The realtor got back in bed. *Kids*, she told herself, *out late and making some kind of senseless battle cry against the world*. She rubbed her fingers against the palm of her hand until it hurt. Then she reached for her phone, squinted in the bright light of it, and opened the poker app.

Henry Thayer was still awake when he heard it. His hearing aids were turned up so he could listen to the late-night show, and when he turned off the TV the screaming voice, echoing outside, made a chill pass over his skin. Thayer hobbled over to the window and pulled open the curtains to see an orange light charging down the center of his street, like a meteor, punching a hole through the atmosphere and burning up.

And the screaming he heard, it came from inside the light. The houses on either side of the street went bright as it passed. Inside that light—Thayer later told his friends down at the diner, he was pretty sure it was fire, a moving, breathing, streak of fire—he could barely make out a human shape. Hunched over, twisting its head from side to side, and screaming as if something were ripping the life right out of it.

The fire came to a sudden stop in the center of the street, and slowly shrank down to nothing until the light went out. The screaming stopped, and the street was so quiet and still that Henry Thayer wondered if he'd simply imagined the whole thing. He sat back down in the recliner. Maybe it was his old eyes and ears playing tricks on him. Or maybe it was the new heart medication his doctor had prescribed. Besides, he was used to strange disruptions at all hours because of that gray house across the street.

Thayer did not call the cops because he could not be sure that what he saw was even real. He worried this day might come, the day when he saw something he didn't *want* to see. Sometimes, especially at night, his dead wife, Alice, would visit him. As clear and vivid as though she were still alive. She would shuffle throughout the house, wearing the slippers and bathrobe she died in, telling Thayer about the phone conversation she'd had with their daughter who lived in Boston.

Thayer knew she wasn't there. Her body was buried in the Catholic cemetery and he left flowers at the headstone every week. But he didn't want Alice to go, so he watched her move from room to room and he counted himself blessed that he got to see her at all.

This was different, though. *But, maybe one comes with the other,* he thought. *Maybe, if you want to see your dead wife, you also have put up with fire flashing through your neighborhood every once in a while.*

It was something Henry Thayer was willing to live with. Until, that is, he heard another voice screaming. This one an old woman's, and not his dead wife's.

Thayer got out of his chair quickly, winced at the grind in his hip, and went to the front door. He opened it and the screaming got louder, but it had changed and now there were tears in it as well, gasping and weeping between each shout of horror.

Thayer recognized the woman in the street dressed in just a nightgown. Like him, Jean Lawson was alone—her husband had died just before Christmas, and Thayer would occasionally visit, do some minor handiwork around the house. But he had never seen her like this. Her husband's death had been a long time coming and surprised no one. And maybe that was why Jean mostly kept it together.

But here she was, standing in the middle of street screaming her head off. One hand clutched the fabric of her nightgown, and the other pointed one arthritic finger at something in the road. From his doorway, Thayer couldn't see what it was, but it had to be something bad.

Thayer groaned as he slipped on his shoes and went outside. The air was frigid and his breath came out of him like smoke. He gripped the cold metal railing as he went carefully down the icy steps. The cold seeped in through his clothes and he wished he'd put on a jacket.

By the time Thayer made it to Jean Lawson, the woman had fallen to her knees near a charred black mass in the street in front of the crumbling gray house everyone on the block despised. Silver smoke rose up from the burned thing, like a campfire that had just been doused with water.

Jean's screaming had stopped, replaced now with an awful whimpering that reminded Thayer of a dog that needed to be let outside.

There was a pungent odor as Thayer got closer, like burnt meat, and the smell made his stomach clench. The thing in the street had a familiar shape, a human shape, but the skin was black and hardened.

Jean Lawson looked up, saw Thayer, and started crying even louder. That one finger kept pointing, shaking like she had Parkinson's. She spoke, but Thayer could not understand a single word. He went over and knelt down next to her, wrapped his arms around her shoulders. Her whole body trembled.

"Take it easy, Jean," Thayer said. "Try and calm down."

The woman lowered her arm and sniffed, let herself lean into Thayer's embrace. Each breath shook and it made Thayer think of when he used to comfort his daughters when they woke up from a nightmare.

"I was asleep," Jean said, "and I heard screaming in a dream. But when I woke up I still heard it…"

"I heard it too," Thayer said.

Jean looked up at him and her eyes got big. "When

I came out there were still flames on him." Her chin quivered. "He was still moving, but then he stopped."

She put her face to Thayer's chest and started crying even harder. This close, there was no question the body was a person, and that smell was nearly overwhelming. Later, Thayer told the cops it was like a burnt pot roast, nauseating, with a sweetly metallic quality to it. It stuck in the back of his throat and made him gag. In fact, he didn't eat meat for several weeks afterward.

But then Thayer saw something that made his hands stop stroking Jean Lawson's bed-messed white hair. He gently pulled himself away from the weeping woman and went closer to the body. The clothes, if it had been wearing any, were gone. So was the hair. The entire corpse was black, except for the teeth, which were bared in a horrifying lipless grin, and the bright-red, wet-looking strips where the skin had split open and exposed the tissue underneath.

It was like something out of those war documentaries he watched on TV, burned bodies strewn across a battlefield. But those images could not have prepared him for the horror of being this close to it in real life, and no way could he ever have imagined the stench.

The legs were pulled up, almost perpendicular to the waist, as though the person had been sitting in a chair. The arms were pulled up toward the chest, the hands twisted into gnarled claws. But it wasn't the body that had made Thayer stand up and walk closer. It was the asphalt underneath it.

The body lay at the center of a black circle, about five or six feet across, and although Thayer was no mathematician, he guessed that if he got his tape measure it would be a perfect circle.

There was nothing else around the body—no fuel, no starter, nothing to make sense of how or why this body had gotten where it was. It was as if it had just fallen from the sky and landed right in the dead center of Archer Way. Thayer actually looked up at the sky like there might be a hole ripped in the clouds.

"What do you see?" Jean asked him. She had managed to get up and was slowly backing away toward the curb.

Thayer looked at her, and held up his hand for her to wait.

Maybe someone had soaked this person in gasoline, then put him in a car, drove here, pushed him out, and threw a match on him. But why hadn't the burning man just thrown himself into the thick snow that covered every lawn?

Thayer shook his head. It didn't make any sense.

The light he'd seen had been moving faster than a person could run, especially while on fire. And why the circle?

That was where Henry Thayer's rational mind hit a dead end, and he started to feel the creeping sensation of the inexplicable crawl up his spine. He had felt like this only two other times in his life: once when he saw a light moving in the sky, too fast to be a plane, and it stopped, changed course, and went zipping off in the opposite direction. That thing, whatever it was, had defied the laws of physics and it left Thayer feeling dizzy and afraid. The second time was right after Alice had passed away. The space above her hospital bed shimmered for a few seconds, like the air above a hot desert road, and that shimmer floated up. The ceiling tiles quivered a little, looked like they were melting, then the shimmer stopped and all was still and quiet.

Thayer felt that again, looking at the charred body in the middle of his street. He was suddenly aware of his heart thumping inside him, beating against his ribs, and his legs went pinpricked and weak.

He turned and walked away, went and sat on the curb next to Jean Lawson, who had a cell phone in her hands.

"I called the police," she said.

Thayer nodded, but said nothing. He stared at that old gray, two-story house. All the windows dark. How many times had he called the cops because of all the people pulling up, going inside, and then stumbling out in the fog of some other world? How he hated that house.

Jean swallowed hard. "I came out here and thought at first this was just a sick joke."

Thayer looked at her, confused.

"I've been having nightmares lately," she said. "Bad ones. Ever since Keith died."

Henry Thayer looked at his neighbor and realized he had never seen her in anything less than nice clothes, hair done up, makeup on, facing the world with a warm smile and a positive attitude. But now, she looked so old. Her hair, as white as dirty snow, stuck up all over the place, and the lines in her face were deep and innumerable. They were the same age but she looked so much older.

Grief will do that, Thayer thought. *Maybe I look the*

same to her.

"You see," Jean said, staring ahead at the burned body, "Keith was cremated. And I've been having these dreams where he wakes up in the furnace and starts screaming at me to let him out. He looks just like that. All burned and black, except he's alive again."

Thayer put his hand over Jean's, squeezed it once, and gave her a smile.

He said, "You know that's just your mind trying to process everything."

"I know," Jean said, "I'm no fool. But then I come out here and see this. Hard not to see a connection."

Just as Thayer heard sirens in the distance, a figure emerged from the dark, walking slowly down the street toward the body. Thayer stood, not sure if this was the person responsible for the burned body. His fingers tightened into a fist.

The figure's walk became a jog, then a run. A cracked voice called out, "Dad?"

As the person got closer Thayer saw it was a young man, high school probably, wearing a hoodie and jeans. This kid's face was completely fallen, every muscle slack.

The kid repeated "Dad" over and over until he

stood next to the charred remains. Then the word fell apart and became weeping. The young man fell to his knees just at the edge of the black circle.

Thayer started to go to him when Archer Way was lit up once again, this time with flashing red and white lights. So he went and sat back down, watched as the paramedics rushed to the body, as the cops gently lifted the kid off his knees and took him to one of their cars.

A breeze blew and scratched dead leaves on the sidewalk. Thayer shivered. He hadn't smoked in over thirty years, but he used to joke with Alice that he'd start up again once she died. She would always laugh and tell him he was more than welcome to hasten his departure to see her. And even though Thayer had no intention of ever sucking on those cancer sticks again, as he sat by Jean Lawson and looked at the remains of a corpse burned beyond recognition, he wanted nothing more than to go home, sit in his recliner, and have a cigarette.

2

Three Months Later

Zach Ayers stood just outside his bedroom window, shoes soaked and toes numb from the snow, head light and spinning from the pills. The whole walk home in the dark he'd felt like his skull was about to lift off his shoulders and go floating into the night.

Each blink of his eyes was slow and heavy, and his hand seemed detached from his body as he held it to the window and pushed. The glass was cold and felt good on his skin. Slowly, the window lifted with a loud creak. Zach stopped and hunched down, heart hammering. His sister, Tessa, slept behind the window just a few feet away, in the room right next to his.

He didn't worry about waking up his mom because she wasn't even home, and wouldn't be for another couple of hours.

Yes, he was in charge of making sure Tessa ate her dinner, did her homework, and got to bed on time. And yes, he'd slipped out in the middle of the night, leaving his sister all alone while he went to a party and got so high he wasn't even sure his feet were actually touching the ground.

When he left the house, after he was good and sure Tessa was really asleep, he went outside into the cool air and something like a fever gripped the back of his neck. But it wasn't a fever, he knew that because he knew the feeling. He had felt it before.

Guilt.

He walked down the street, knowing full well that if something happened to his sister he would never forgive himself, if he could even live with himself. Scenarios ran through his head—the house catching fire, someone breaking in and kidnapping Tessa, her waking up, finding no one home, and wandering outside to find help.

The thoughts made Zach sick, but something in him, even deeper, made him sicker. A need just burning a hole right through the center of his chest. So he kept walking, each step farther from the house a little nail in the coffin that held his conscience.

But he couldn't stop. Not until he had what he needed. One quick stop before the party.

He took out his cell phone and texted Hazard that he was on his way.

Back at home now, just as the dark sky grew lighter, Zach crouched outside his window and listened for footsteps, for any sign that the creak had woken Tessa up. The house was quiet, so he stood and lifted the window a little more, wincing at the screech it made, then grabbed the sill and hoisted himself up. But he couldn't really feel his hands and he fell back into the snow, right on his ass. What he did feel was the cold wetness soaking through his jeans.

He dug his fingers into the snow and held them there until they tingled. Now his hands were something his brain was aware of. Zach stood back up, grabbed the sill again, and managed to pull his upper body into the bedroom, but that's where his strength gave out.

With his legs still hanging outside, Zach thought he knew what being paralyzed must feel like, and he started to laugh because he imagined his soul slipping out of his body, stepping back and looking at the situation confused as hell. He buried his mouth in his arm and tried to laugh quietly, but he wasn't really laughing because it was so funny. His brain was just sparking, and it kind of scared him that he didn't want to laugh, to make noise, but he couldn't seem to stop.

Stuck, folded in half over the window, blood rushed to Zach's head and pressure gathered behind his eyes until they started to water. His numb fingers reached out and touched the carpet. Using his fingertips, Zach pulled himself inch by inch into his bedroom. He tried to ease his legs in gracefully, but they just thumped limply to the floor.

He lay there breathing heavily and staring up at the ceiling. The walls came loose and began to slowly move in a circle around him (like that ride at the fair that spins so fast you get pushed against the wall as the floor drops beneath you), blurring the posters into smears of color. From inside this mess a shape started to emerge—a nose, a mouth, deep-set eyes—and Zach held his breath as this face floated in the air in front of him. It was a face he knew, a face he desperately missed every moment of every day. He felt tears sliding down his skin, itching into his ears.

Zach Ayers closed his eyes but the spinning didn't stop. Even in the blackness he felt the motion and it made him sick. He put one hand on his stomach like it would help hold the vomit in. His other hand twisted into the carpet fibers and held on, as if the gravity in his room would switch off at any second.

He kept his eyes closed and spun into oblivion.

3

Something hammered at Zach's bedroom door and he jerked awake. He sat up fast and it took the room a moment to catch up. His head wasn't light anymore, in fact, it was the opposite, a weight so heavy he feared it might snap right off his neck.

Daylight and frigid air came in through the still-open window. His muscles ached as he got to his knees and looked at the clock on the nightstand. Good, still early.

He got to his feet and staggered to the door. He unlocked it and found Tessa standing there in her pajamas, head cocked to the side, one hand on her hip. Her eyes looked him up and down. Their mother's eyes, dark and piercing. Their eyes met and all her confidence, the attitude, just dissolved.

Her face fell and she looked down at the floor.

"I won't tell Mom you left," she said. "But if you ever leave me here on my own again, I will tell. And I don't think she'd ever forgive you."

Tessa shifted her weight to the other leg and crossed her arms.

"I'm taking a shower," she said. "And you better do something about this," waving a hand at him, "before Mom gets home."

She turned and her tight, black curls bounced down the hall into the bathroom. The door shut, harder than it needed to, and soon the water started and the pipes clanged in the walls.

Zach went over to the mirror above his dresser and looked at the person in the glass. The skin under his eyes was dark and swollen, but the eyes themselves were bright red. Twigs and dead leaves were stuck in his hair, and there were mud stains all over his clothes, not to mention all over the carpet where he'd slept.

His head pulsed with each heartbeat and he could

only hope that he felt good enough to fake it by the time Mom got off work. She started working the night shift at the hospital after Dad because of the differential, couple dollars more an hour for working when no sane person wanted to work. And what did she do all night? Pushed a mop around to clean up the blood, shit, and piss from a hundred sick people. Thankless, filthy work that left her exhausted and smelling of disinfectant when she finally came home.

She had been so much happier before Dad...

Those words pushed into Zach's gut like something sharp.

Before Dad.

Before Dad died, left them, passed away. However Zach phrased it didn't do the actual thing justice.

He shook his head to clear the thoughts, but they still lingered like when he used to try and get the smell of cigarette smoke out of his room before his parents came in—window open, Ferris-wheeling his arms to move the air—but it never worked.

He took off his clothes and threw them in the hamper, then slipped on the cleanest T-shirt and pair of jeans from off the floor. Once Tessa was out of the shower he'd rinse his hair and put on some deodorant, hope Mom was too tired to take a really good look at him.

When he went over to the bed his legs felt strange, like he was walking through thick snow, an astronaut on the surface of some distant planet. The motion made his stomach sick, and he tried to remember how many pills he'd taken yesterday.

Zach had always believed that people with "problems," like his dad, didn't even know how far they'd slipped away from the real, the normal. Now, Zach wondered if he'd been wrong about that. He knew he was getting worse, could feel it every day. But he couldn't stop, couldn't come up for air long enough to admit to his mom that he needed help.

He knelt down and put his face to the carpet, seeing dark burn spots from the ash of the joints he used to smoke more frequently, before Hazard gave him the pills.

With a burn spot scratching at his face, Zach reached one arm under the bed and searched until his fingers touched the cold metal of his Superman lunch box. He pulled it out and held it for a moment. He still remembered what it had looked like before the paint started to wear off, how much he loved it as a kid. He'd take that thing out at school and believe it said something about him, sent a signal to all the other kids that this, this hero was someone he aspired to be.

Now look at you, he thought.

Zach heard the water of the shower turn off, knew Tessa would be coming out any minute, so he took a breath and lifted the creaky lid. Inside was one wrinkled dollar bill and a small baggie with two orange pills.

Shit. He knew he'd been taking a lot over the last week, but in the cotton fog of his brain he had forgotten just how much of his stash he'd burned through. Two wouldn't even be enough for the day ahead. And as far as money went, he was looking at the last of it.

Money.

That's what Mom and Dad had been fighting about the night Dad died. Mom had hid his keys and Dad was screaming at her, pounding his hand on the dresser in their bedroom so hard the autopsy x-rays later showed he'd fractured it. But Mom stood her ground, said she wouldn't let him drive, so Dad left the house and Zach watched from the window as he went down the street with his glitchy walk, still arguing with someone who wasn't there. Something dropped from Zach's chest down to his guts as Dad vanished into the night, and sometimes he still had dreams of running after him. Dreams in which he was forever chasing someone who could not be seen, calling his name into the dark.

Next time Zach saw Dad he was burned beyond recognition on Archer Way, then his cracked face in the ambulance with a tube down his throat. A paramedic squeezed a bag and Dad's chest rose. An IV in his arm dripped meds that Dad would have loved had he been awake to feel them.

Already gone, but they just had to go through the motions.

Zach shook his head and glanced over at the clock. No time for a shower before Mom got home. He grabbed the baggie, took out one pill, snapped it in half to make it hit faster, and put the pieces under his tongue. A bitter, chalky taste filled his mouth. Each heartbeat was so clear Zach thought he could feel the muscle quiver beneath his ribs as it pushed blood throughout his body. His hands got shaky, like after too much coffee and not enough food.

Every time the pills wore off he couldn't help wondering what Mom would think if she saw him, and that filled him with a guilt so heavy it nearly buckled his knees, and the only thing that would take away the guilt was another pill. But it didn't really take it away, did it? Hid it for a while, maybe, but it was always there, waiting for him when he resurfaced from the slow-motion world.

Fifteen minutes, that's how long it usually took for the morphine to hit. And when it did, it hit fast.

But before then he had to get cleaned up. He decided he didn't want Mom to think he wasn't ready for the day, ready to get Tessa on the bus and get himself to school. Normally he'd ride his bike, but he sold it three weeks ago for cash and told Mom it had been stolen. She believed him, just like she always did, at least Zach thought so. But maybe she knew and was just too tired to throw herself in front of the wreck he was making of his own life. Maybe what he thought of as belief was actually apathy.

The bathroom door opened and Tessa came out humming. Zach grabbed the hoodie that hung from his desk chair, held it to his nose, and sniffed. Good, it didn't smell like cigarette or weed smoke. He put that on and then dug through the closet to find a pair of shoes that weren't covered in mud.

Through the wall he and Tessa shared, Zach heard his sister singing along to some awful pop music as she got dressed and did her hair. It was the same routine every morning, but this time he stopped and listened. Her voice didn't sound like it belonged to an eleven-year-old girl—there was something in the tone of it, in the way she shaped each note, that sounded like someone much older. Someone who had lived life, experienced heartache. Zach's eyes burned.

If you can't be better for her, then who?

Thoughts, so clear and simple, formed in his mind. Mom and Tessa, they were all he had in the world. How could he not be more for them?

Zach wiped his bloodshot eyes and went over to the door, put his hand on the knob. He wanted to see her, give her a hug, say he loved her, but his eyes fluttered as his head grew lighter, and all those thoughts burst apart in chalky explosions. He felt each one dissolve like a pill under the tongue.

All those things he wanted to say, the things he wanted to be, all washed away under a wave of medication. Zach swayed, his hand still on the knob, and it kept him from falling over. He couldn't even remember what he had been doing, but he knew it was important and that made his eyes burn even more.

He closed his eyes and let the wave move through him, erase the pain, the uncertainty, until all he could think was *I don't want this feeling to end.*

4

The front door of the house opened and a vibration moved through the walls when it closed. The metallic sound of keys being tossed on the countertop. Zach opened his mouth, stretched it as wide as it would go. He smiled big and felt like his lips were melting right off his face. He tried to blink fast but his eyelids closed so slowly it felt like falling asleep.

He rummaged through his bedside table, found a package of mints, and popped one. Then he put on his shoes and opened his bedroom door. He went down the hall, and Tessa's voice, still singing, followed him all the way to the kitchen.

He heard the water running before he entered the room, heard the clink of things going into the dishwasher, the scrape of a sponge. Guilt sounded like a distant alarm in his mind. He had promised Mom to clean the kitchen before she got home. Promised to take out the trash and vacuum the living room so she wouldn't have to worry about it. But he hadn't done any of those things. Instead, he had waited until Tessa was asleep, even crept into her room and listened for her breathing, before crawling out his window so the neighbor across the street, who watched TV late into the night with his curtains open, wouldn't see him.

Zach breathed deep and came into the kitchen. Mom hunched over the sink, still in her hospital issued scrubs—blue top and gray pants—scraping crusted food off a plate Zach himself had left on the counter. One plate of many. His empty soda cans were scattered all over the living room, the kitchen. She wore yellow rubber gloves, and Zach thought about how she wore gloves all night at work to clean up after other people. Now, she came home and traded hospital gloves for dish gloves.

The muscles in his mom's thin arms worked hard

as she scrubbed. Strands of hair, white as a pill and fine as sewing thread, came loose from her hair band and hung over her eyes. There had been no white hair before Dad's long dark fall into a long dark night, and her eyes didn't have that sagging flesh underneath them. Eyes that seemed to sink farther back into her head and stare out from inside burrowed holes. Zach watched her, and somewhere beneath that wave of numbing bliss, his heart ached.

She looked up when she sensed his presence, but she didn't stop scrubbing. With her jaw clenched, Mom stared straight at her son with narrowed eyes and scrubbed harder, little droplets of sweat glistening on her upper lip. Zach knew the look. If he'd been six years old she'd be reaching for the nearest wooden spoon to paddle his butt. Even through the morphine fog he knew he had to fix this. He just wasn't sure how.

He tried to think of something to say. His tongue took up too much space in his mouth, and it was numb like after getting a shot of Novocain at the dentist.

"Where did you go last night?" Mom said.

Zach's heart beat a little faster. He blinked and his eyes wanted to stay closed. He struggled to open them back up.

"Nowhere," he said, and tried to smile. "I was here."

Mom eyes filled with water until it looked like she wore liquid contact lenses. Her hands gripped the edge of the counter. Her chin shook as she glanced around the room at all the things Zach should have done, but didn't.

"Do you think I'm stupid?" she asked.

Zach opened his mouth, but Mom said, "It used to be impossible for you to lie to me. When did that change?"

"I was here," Zach said, and the morphine moved through him, told him that this unfolding moment wasn't quite real, even though his shallow heartbeat told him it *was* real, and it mattered.

Veins bulged in Mom's arms as her hands tightened on the edge of the counter. Her voice came out in a hoarse whisper.

"There are footprints in the snow leading right to your window," she said. "A window that's still open."

Her nostrils flared and she spoke through clenched teeth.

"You left your sister here by herself, in the middle of the night. What if something had happened to her?" Mom swallowed and made a face like someone had punched her in the stomach. "And you come stumbling out here like I won't know what you're doing. I trusted you, Zach."

All those tears that filled Mom's eyes broke loose and ran down her face. She closed her eyes tight and her shoulders moved up and down with silent sobbing. Zach wanted to go to her, to put his arms around her and apologize, tell her he was sorry and he'd do better.

Just then, a door closed and Tessa came down the hall, her backpack jingling with a dozen keychains, still humming her song, and Zach went a little weak behind the knees as Mom stood up straight and held out her arms to Tessa, her whole face transforming into a beautiful, tired smile.

Mom said, "Hey sweetie," and held Tessa's head to her chest. "Did you have breakfast?"

Tessa's big brown eyes shifted, came to rest on her brother, and she said, "Yeah, I had a banana and some yogurt."

The guilt, if that's what it was, changed shape, sharpened, and dug even further into Zach's side. She lied for him. The obnoxious little beast had covered for him. Breakfast was supposed to be his responsibility, and he had neglected it just like he neglected everything else. His heart felt heated with love and hurt all at the same time.

Mom closed her eyes and patted Tessa's back, and she looked so tired Zach thought she might fall asleep with her chin resting in Tessa's still-wet hair.

"Good," she said. "Better get on out there before the bus comes."

Tessa moved back and Mom gave her a kiss on the forehead. "Go on," she said.

Once Tessa was outside, and the door slammed behind her, Mom went right back to cleaning dishes, the faucet as loud as a waterfall in Zach's head. The whole room was filled with his mom's anger, disappointment, pain—whatever, it was suffocating. Zach moved from one foot to the other.

"Mom," he said, "I was going to—"

"Shh." She held up one hand, a fork gripped in her fingers, soapy water running down the yellow gloves to her arm. "Don't say another word."

Her head lifted slowly until she looked straight at him, and if Zach had never met her before he would think there was no love in those eyes at all.

"You tell me everything I need to know without even speaking," she said. She opened her mouth, closed it, and her eyes filled with tears again. She tried to speak again and her mouth twisted up. The fork fell from her hand to the sink with a clatter.

She held up one finger. "You are not the only one who lost your father. You are not the only one in pain."

Zach tried to take a step backward but the floor had turned into something not solid and he stumbled a little. Mom shook her head and put the soapy hand to her mouth.

"How could you do this to me, Zach?"

Zach tried to make himself go to her and he stumbled again, closed his eyes for what felt like too long, and when he opened them Mom's arm was held straight out, pointing to the front door. Her eyes stared at his chest, as if trying to see if there was a heart beating somewhere in there.

"I can't even look at you," she said. "Get out of my house."

Zach held up a hand, reached for her. "Mom, I—"

"Now." Her voice was firm, but she still wouldn't look into his eyes.

Things in the room, the refrigerator and stove, the table and chairs, and Mom herself, lost definition, became fuzzy and see-through. Even the particles in the floor seemed to separate, to become gaps he could fall into. Zach took a step toward the door and felt his body tip with the motion. He continued to hold his hand out for balance, but also because he wasn't quite sure where the room ended and objects began. When his fingers touched wood, he searched for the knob, found it, and pulled open the front door. With one hand on the cold metal railing, so cold it burned his skin, Zach made it to the walkway and then to the sidewalk. He stopped, looked back, and saw the still ghostly shape of his mother walking down the hall to her bedroom. The door closed and the house filled with the white noise of the sound machine she used to help her sleep during the day. Even through that oceanlike static he could hear her crying, a broken sound that twisted in his guts. A sound he had heard so often since Dad died that Zach thought he'd gotten used to it.

But this was different. Mom's gasping cries were not because of Dad, or work, or money. They were because of him. Of all the pain she had been through, this brokenness was his fault and it made sharp thoughts grow in his mind. And he knew only one way to dull them.

Zach started walking, slowly at first, but the frigid

air brought the world back into a solid form and he knew exactly where he was going.

5

Each house was in worse shape than the last. Weather beaten with paint curling off the siding, and sagging roofs covered in moss. Zach went past a house where every window was blocked with mold-stained curtains. Past another with a car parked in the driveway that had been there as long as he could remember. Tires flattened into a puddle of black rubber, actual weeds growing out of the silt that covered the hood. Another house with sun-bleached baby toys abandoned in the yard, sprouting up out of the snow like some kind of strange flowers.

The houses made Zach feel bad, like his head was

tuned into the static between radio stations. He couldn't help wondering how many of these houses had a mom just like his, trying to sleep off a long shift before getting up to put in another. And how many had a kid just like him, walking the streets with a pill clouding up his bloodstream? That made his head ache even worse and he shook it to clear the thought, but that just made him queasy.

Zach shivered and shoved both hands deep into the pockets of his sweatshirt. He wished he had a coat and beanie to keep him warm. His breath came out and trailed behind him like the steam from a train. This thought made him laugh a little and he said, "Choo choo" out loud, but the sound of his own voice was strange and distant.

He could take a right down Crescent Drive and cut across over to Hazard's, but that would mean going down Archer, and that was the last place in the world Zach wanted to be.

Archer Way.

That's where the house was. The gray, two-story house that looked like it had been transported from somewhere in the South and dumped on an empty lot here in Portland. Plantation style, his mom called it, which always made him think of slaves. But it did have that look with those big columns that held up the small second-story porch. Vines wrapped around the columns and climbed up to the roof. A roof that bent down so far it was a wonder a crack hadn't opened up in all those tiles.

That house.

The house that killed his dad.

Because Zach never saw who lived there, the person who gave Dad the drugs, Zach always thought of the house as a thing, an entity that chewed people up and spit them back out dazed and drooling, pupils constricted to pinpoints. Zach couldn't think of the gray house without seeing Dad's body lying on the street, his charred and blackened corpse. He hated that he'd seen Dad like that, and he blamed God that he had to see it over and over again, almost every single night.

The nightmares Zach Ayers had were made up of his own memories. Twisted together, stretched out, exaggerated, and projected right into his subconscious with all the sound and color of a movie.

He kept walking. He'd take the long way to Hazard's.

He turned onto Palm Street and passed a falling-apart house with so many cars parked in the driveway that several were all the way on the lawn. He recognized at least two of them. They drove by his house all the time, low bass rattling the window in his room.

Music thumped from inside the house and he heard loud voices talking, yelling. Somewhere in all that sound was a baby crying. Zach stopped, listened. The crying was frantic, a high-pitched wail that shook with fear, or anger. The kind of wailing that was impossible to ignore. The sound tensed all the muscles in Zach's neck and he pictured some chubby infant, diaper full to bursting, hands balled into fists, screaming with all its strength for someone to pick him up, hold him.

Zach leaned into the sound, the crying, wishing someone would make it stop. But it just kept going, and Zach made his heavy legs start moving again. It felt wrong to just walk by, like he should do something, but what could he do? Knock on the front door and stand there shivering as it opened up to a room full of people so distant from the world that even the shrieks of a child couldn't pull them away? What then?

Zach walked until he could no longer hear the cries, or the music, and soon the house was forgotten. He took out his phone and sent Hazard a text.

Coming over. You home?

Up ahead, a slow-moving blue and white car pulled onto the street, coming in Zach's direction. Zach's breath caught in his throat when he saw the light bar on the roof and the words "Portland Police" stenciled on the doors.

Zach put his head down and kept walking, feeling a burning on his scalp as the cop car came closer. Zach kept his hands in his pockets and tried to walk normally. He didn't look up, didn't acknowledge the cop. He knew how quickly getting stopped by the police could turn into getting killed.

The car crawled by and the cop turned toward Zach, staring straight at him through the window. The man's bald head was as smooth and shiny as a polished stone, and his eyes were hidden behind big black sunglasses. His lips were pressed so tightly together that his mouth was just a thin line, his face unreadable. The cop's skull looked scooped in on either side of the forehead, giving him an inhuman appearance.

When the car passed, Zach took one quick look behind him and saw it come to stop. It pulled a U-turn in the middle of the street and started driving down the opposite side, right behind Zach. The car matched his pace, followed close enough for Zach to hear the engine, the squeak of the wipers as they flung fat snowflakes off the windshield.

Zach's legs moved faster.

The phone buzzed in his pocket, but no way was he pulling it out right now.

He felt pressure on the back of his head, two small circles of heat, like the cop's eyes were burning through Zach's skull and searching through all the thoughts and memories in there.

He knows. He knows where I'm going.

Zach started walking a little faster.

His shoulders bunched up and he expected to hear the *whoop-whoop* of the siren at any second, telling him to stop, to put his hands up. And the questions, there would be so many questions he couldn't answer. In fact, Zach didn't know if he could talk even if he wanted to. His tongue felt too big for his mouth, and it was so dry, scraping over his teeth as he tried to work up some saliva.

He shivered again as sweat slid down his back.

Fear made his legs weak, made the skin behind his knees tingle. He looked over at the house to his right, saw his distorted reflection in one window, and the warped cop car in the glass of the other window.

The cop, with his completely hairless head and black glasses, looked almost like an insect and that gave Zach another reason to be afraid. He couldn't be sure there even was a cop car following him. With his head floating, barely attached to his shoulders, it wouldn't be the first time Zach had seen something that wasn't really there, or that the morphine changed a real thing into something grotesque and strange.

The tires made a squishing sound as they rolled through slush that had collected along the curb. The engine clicked.

Zach felt the salt sting of sweat as it ran into his eyes. It dripped down his neck, his chest.

He looked up. Thick snowflakes drifted out of a gray sky and touched his face. His heart beat so hard he couldn't catch his breath. He waited until he heard the sound of the car engine change as it came to a stop. And when he heard the creak of the door open, Zach pulled his hands out of his pockets and took off running as fast as he could.

6

Zach's shoes pounded the concrete in time to the pulsing in his head. When he came to the next street he took a sharp right, jumped over a low wall of bushes and cut through the yard of the house on the corner. By the time his lungs started to burn, the cop car was out of sight and Zach found himself on a street he had no memory of ever walking down. Tall tress lined either side, their long branches stretching out and creating a thick canopy over the street.

It was colder here, darker.

Zach stopped, looked behind him. There was no

cop, no siren in the distance. The street was silent except for the creak of tree branches. Nothing moved. The cars parked along each curb were covered in snow, as though they'd been parked for days.

Zach took the phone out of his pocket and saw a reply from Hazard.

Knock three times.

He kept moving, taking quick backward glances to make sure he wasn't being followed. The houses he passed, on the left and the right, none of them had any lights on. The whole street was dark and quiet, and Zach had the uneasy feeling that the houses were not empty. That there were things inside each home, watching him.

The branches above him swayed in a high breeze and clumps of snow fell to the ground with the sound of a fist hitting a body. He went by one house, then another. Each of them silent and dark. The yards and walkways were covered in unbroken snow. No footprints, not even paw prints. The only sound was the crunch of snow as he walked.

Halfway down the street, Zach paused and looked at a gray two-story house with pillars on the front porch. It looked just like the house on Archer Way, only as it might have looked before it fell into ruin. But still, it was just similar enough to make Zach's heart trip over a beat.

He turned to keep walking but saw something move in an upstairs window. He took a couple steps up the walkway, squinting at the glass. From the corner a small, misshapen black face came into view. Its staring eyes surrounded by stark white circles. Two points at the top of the head looked like horns.

Zach yelled out and backed away so fast his feet lost traction and he almost went down. His arms pinwheeled to right himself, and when he looked again he saw a black and white cat slinking along the window sill, staring at him with watchful eyes.

Hunched over, Zach laughed and tried to catch his breath. The cat moved to the other side of the sill then jumped down out of view.

Zach started moving and wished again that he hadn't sold his bike. It hadn't been a really fancy bike, just a Ricochet "Hollow Point," but he had worked bagging groceries to save the money to buy it. Dad had refused to pay for it, said it would feel different if Zach was the one to earn it. And Dad was right. It did feel different. It felt more *his*.

But sometimes Zach wondered if he had really earned every dollar he spent on the bike, because sometimes, Zach would open up his Superman lunchbox, where he kept his money, and find just a little more cash in it than he remembered having. At the time, he told himself he probably just miscounted, but he knew better. And later, when Mom and Dad thought he and Tessa were asleep, they'd start fighting about money. Zach knew enough to understand Dad had good days and bad days, and if cash ended up in the lunchbox it meant Dad hadn't spent it at the gray house on Archer. And that was a good day. After a while, those days stopped coming, but every time Zach rode his bike he knew that they existed in the past, and they could exist again in the future.

He rode that bike for three years before deciding to turn it back into money. And then he dissolved that money under his tongue.

Sometimes, when the pills were just beginning to wear off, Zach had these thoughts that sparked in his brain like a cigarette lighter almost out of fluid. Crystal-clear ideas about the world, his life. The future seemed like something close enough to touch, but fragile enough to break like glass if he made the wrong choice. And that was something he could never understand, why mistakes were always easier to make than something good, something right.

He couldn't wait to get to Hazard's, pop something, anything, and drown out these thoughts, numb all those sparking wires.

Farther down the quiet street, frozen in time it felt like, Zach reached an intersection and turned around. His mouth went even more dry, and his tongue felt made of sand. Most of the houses were all lit up, warm yellow light spilling from the windows onto the snow. A man in a fuzzy blue coat walked his dog and waved at a neighbor walking hers. The two-story gray house, like the one on Archer Way, still had multicolored Christmas lights wrapped around the porch pillars.

Zach closed his eyes as his equilibrium shut off and on, and he wasn't sure he could keep standing. He started to lower himself to the ground when the hiss of white noise came into his head. The sound of ocean waves coming into shore. He opened his eyes just as a car pulled onto the street, down in the direction he had just come from. He couldn't see clearly, his vision had gone blurry, but he thought he saw a smooth head with black eyes in the driver's seat.

He straightened up and took a quick left at the intersection, hoping the cop hadn't seen him, and immediately recognized some of the houses on this street. He actually wasn't that far from where he'd been last night, at the party. A few blocks farther and he'd be able to see Hazard's apartment building rising up in the distance. He'd be safe if he could just make it there.

Zach breathed deep and started walking faster.

7

Zach looked back every few steps expecting to see the cop car coming around the corner, the serpentine head of the man driving it aiming those black eyes at Zach's thoughts. He didn't know what he was so afraid of. They couldn't test him for drugs right there on the street, and he wasn't doing anything but walking. And no cop could force him to say where he was going, or what he was going to do when he got there. But still, he couldn't shake the feeling that the cop knew, saw Zach's purpose flickering on his brain like a movie on a screen.

The closer Zach got to the apartment complex,

and no flashing lights came tearing down the street, the more he relaxed.

A few kids were playing just outside the building, shooting a faded basketball into a hoop with no net. Old enough to be in school, they probably had parents up in those apartments who were passed out and drooling with a needle still stuck in their arms. Parents who would never even know whether or not their kids went to class.

Zach recognized a couple of them, but not by name. He nodded as he passed, and they nodded back. Zach had always loved basketball. When did that change? Was it when Dad stopped showing up to games even though he promised he'd be there? Or was it after Dad died, when Zach couldn't see the point of throwing a ball around a gym while everything certain in his life had been incinerated? When he woke up every day unable to move because of a pain so deep it seemed to have settled inside his bones? Or was it after he met Hazard and got the pills, the only thing that made all the dark, empty space inside him feel less hollow? He still missed the game, though. Sometimes. And he did right now. Some part of him wanted to walk over to the kids, clap his hands together twice for the ball, and show them how it was done. But the other need was louder, and Zach kept walking.

He climbed the stairwell, took note of some new tags spray-painted on the wall. So new and clear the paint still looked wet. A woman's screams echoed down to him, then a man's voice screaming back. Doors slammed, someone ran. Footsteps pounded, vibrating the stairs under his feet.

He stopped at the third-floor landing and looked down into the courtyard. The swimming pool had been drained last year and never filled back up. Hazard said there was a crack in the concrete too expensive to fix. It had become something of a garbage dump since then. People threw broken things from their balconies, watched them smash into the pool. TVs, microwaves, furniture, even old food. A layer of snow and dead leaves covered most of it, but Zach could still smell it. Hazard said management would probably just fill it with cement in the spring.

At the fifth floor, Zach passed doors that were scarred and tagged. Some of the brass numbers were missing, leaving faded ghost numbers. TVs blared from either side of the hall. One voice yelled for the other person to turn theirs down, then that person yelled the same thing back. Farther down, music thumped from one room while someone with slurred speech tried to rap along to the beat.

Zach reached the end of the hall, Apartment 5-J, and knocked three times. He waited, heard movement from the other side, the sound of four deadbolts sliding back, then the door opened until the chain caught and an eye peered out through the crack.

"Hello, Zach," Hazard said.

The door closed, the chain clinked loose, and the door reopened. Hazard stood in his "uniform," really the only thing Zach had ever seen him wear—a three-piece gray wool suit, brown leather shoes that matched the brown leather gloves, and a white surgical mask. He poked his head out, looked left and right, put a hand on Zach's shoulder, and pulled him inside. Hazard shut the door and spun all the deadbolts back into place.

They stood on a large, black rubber mat. Hazard pointed down at the row of slippers with red designs stitched onto the top. Japanese symbols, Zach guessed. He knew the drill. He took off his shoes, carefully placed them near the door, and put on a pair of slippers.

"I didn't expect to see you so soon," Hazard said. His blonde hair was combed perfectly and held in place with something that made it shine.

Zach smiled but he didn't find it funny. In fact,

that hard knot in his stomach told him the situation was anything but funny.

His eyes slowly adjusted. The lamp that hung above the dining room table cast a dull yellow light. The floors were a reddish-brown wood, or something like it, and absolutely spotless. They always were. In fact, Zach had never seen such a clean place. Not even the hospital where Mom worked. There were always some pieces of dust lurking in the corners, but not here.

Zach followed Hazard past the kitchen and into the living room. Zach guessed the landlord wasn't aware that Hazard had torn up all the carpet and installed the floors, but then Zach also guessed the landlord was paid a little more than rent each month.

The rumors were that Hazard never left his apartment, ever, that he was a germaphobe. No one Zach knew had ever seen Hazard in the outside world. They said he had his groceries delivered, that the lights in his place were UV. They said he didn't care much for people, and he only wanted to spend time with the characters in his movies. A girl Zach met at a party said Hazard had seen every single movie made up to 1970. He didn't care about anything made after that year.

The TV, which took up most of one wall, was glowing with a black and white image frozen on the screen.

Hazard went to the coffee table and picked up a smoldering pipe from its stand, moved the corner of his mask with one gloved finger and held the pipe between his teeth. An old pipe, like the ones they smoked in old movies, filled with fragrant tobacco. As best as Zach could tell, Hazard didn't take any of the stuff he sold. Which was another dichotomy Zach sometimes struggled to reconcile. How someone could be two such opposite things.

Hazard pointed at the TV with the pipe. "*Turn Up the Sun*, have you seen it?"

Zach shook his head.

"1957," Hazard said, "directed by Hugh Wakefield. This is the part where the private investigator figures out he was hired to find a man who doesn't really exist."

Hazard replaced the pipe and smoke curled from around the mask. "He was hired to become the man he was looking for."

On either side of the living room were long bookshelves made of wood even darker than the floors. One wall held nothing but books, and the other was filled with movie cases. Blu-rays, DVDs, VHS, even some

LaserDiscs. Hundreds, if not thousands of movies.

Zach didn't know much about furniture, other than if it looked expensive it was probably expensive. And everything about Hazard's apartment said *money*. It reminded Zach of a library in one of those old English estates you saw in movies. A place where men gather to smoke cigars and talk politics.

On the other walls hung framed photographs that looked like stills from a film noir. A brick building with a woman's shadow. An alleyway lit by a single streetlamp. A Ferris wheel at night.

Hazard picked up the remote and pointed it at the screen. The frozen image on the TV began moving again. Hazard once told Zach that he had a movie on all day, every day. He picked one film and played it on a loop from the time he woke up until he went to sleep.

Zach tried to act cool, but he couldn't stop himself from looking at the long table against the far wall. A table with ornate carvings around each leg.

Hazard put the pipe down and squinted at Zach. "You seem anxious."

"No, I'm good," Zach said. "Just had a cop following me when I left the house."

Hazard's blue eyes narrowed.

"I ditched him a few blocks back," Zach added, quickly.

"Law enforcement," Hazard said, shaking his head. "Only in a society of slaves is it a crime to free your consciousness."

On the coffee table, next to the pipe, were three cell phones, all different colors. The screen on the one in the middle lit up and vibrated. Hazard picked it up, typed a message.

"Did you hear about Carlos?" he asked.

Zach drifted closer to the long table. A table covered with rows of plastic containers filled with Ziploc bags.

"What about him?" Zach said.

Each bag was filled with pills of all different sizes, shapes, and colors. A few containers had bags with powder.

Hazard typed another message, looked up, and said, "They found his body over on Archer. He had been lit on fire, incinerated. They had to use dental records to identify him. The watch he wore was melted right into the bones of his wrist."

Zach's stomach dropped at the mention of Archer Way, and it dropped even further at the word "fire."

"What was he doing on Archer?" Zach asked.

Another buzz, this time from one of the other phones. Hazard picked that one up, sent a reply, and said, "What does anyone do on that street? They're going after the dark stuff."

Zach knew better than to touch any of the baggies. Hazard's system of arrangement was as meticulous as his cleaning. Taped to the front of each plastic container was a hand-drawn symbol. One had a triangle inside a circle, another a square inside a hexagon. Shapes within shapes. Only Hazard knew what each one meant, a code he claimed he had never written down. It was all in his head. And since so many of the pills were white and round, you needed Hazard to get you what you wanted, otherwise you might end up with blood-pressure meds instead of Vicodin.

"Tony called this morning," Hazard said, "told me what happened. He was very distraught. Crying so hard I could hardly understand him."

Hazard didn't just sell the stuff that sent your mind spinning into multicolored visions of another dimension. He also sold all kinds of medications at discount rates to people who didn't have insurance. But it wasn't an act of charity, a drug was a drug to him. If it was manufactured by a pharmaceutical company, Hazard could probably get it.

"Carlos obviously crossed some very bad people," Hazard said, setting down the phone. "The only reason to set someone on fire in the middle of a street is to make sure everyone sees it. Make sure everyone knows what you're willing to do."

Zach had only seen Carlos two or three times, was introduced at one party or another. Just a guy, walking around with a red plastic cup, acting tough with his friends and cool with the ladies. There was not a single thing he did or said that stood out in Zach's mind. Still, the fact they'd met at all made his death seem somehow more real.

Hazard came over, blinked a few times, and shook his head. "Enough talk about the departed." He waved a hand at the table. "What'll it be today?"

Zach's answer was always the same. He thought that maybe if he didn't do the same stuff as his dad, the "dark stuff" as Hazard called it, maybe he wouldn't be the same as Dad. That was Hazard's logic too, the reason he didn't sell anything unless it could be prescribed by a doctor.

Zach pointed at the container with the circle inside

a triangle. The one with the baggies of orange pills.

Hazard stepped back, angled his head, and looked at Zach through squinted eyes.

He said, "I think you may need something else, Zach, something that doesn't drag you down. Try something that will pick you up, give you some energy."

If there was anyone who could understand why Zach didn't want anything else, it was probably Hazard. But Zach couldn't bring himself to say it out loud. Couldn't say that those other meds made his thoughts race through his brain like a train on a fire. And they didn't even touch the pain—if anything, they made it sharper. He saw himself too clearly with anything else.

"I just want the world to be out of focus, you know?" Zach said.

Hazard nodded, but he kept staring until Zach felt uncomfortable.

The white fabric of his surgical mask moved when he spoke. "Far be it from me to dissuade a valued customer," Hazard said. "You want what you want."

Hazard took one of the plastic baggies and held it out, then put out his other gloved hand, palm up, creased brown leather. Zach reached into his back pocket and took out the wallet he knew was empty. He opened it, hissed "shit," and started digging through his pockets.

"Shit, man" he said. "I forgot to bring the money."

Hazard's fingers closed around the baggie and his hand lowered. The skin between his eyebrows folded.

"No cash, no meds," he said.

Zach nodded. "Look, man, I'm really sorry. I hate to even ask this, but can't you just hook me up now and I'll bring the money in a couple hours?"

Nothing in Hazard's expression changed as one hand went behind his back and came out holding a gun. It hung there at his side, black and shiny. It made Zach think of the rattlesnake he'd seen on a field trip to Smith Rocks. Something poised and unmoving, but dangerous. Ready to strike.

Hazard's voice was low and measured. The mask moved as he spoke. "You know how this works. If you can get the money in a couple hours, that's when you can have the meds. Not until then."

Zach's fist clenched around his wallet. Sweat slicked his palms until the leather became slippery. There was still enough morphine in his system to keep the fear held down, but what scared him most was not the gun, it was what happened when the morphine wore off and he didn't have any more.

Zach held up his hands on instinct and Hazard's blue eyes stared, unblinking.

He turned the gun up, as if showing it to Zach. "You know what this is, right? It's for fools. You're not a fool, Zach. Never have been. Don't turn into one. This stuff," he waved the gun at the table, "can unlock doors in your mind. Or," he shrugged, "it can turn a person into someone they never wanted to be."

Every visible line in Hazard's face, above the mask, went smooth and his expression became stone. The gun turned slowly until it pointed at Zach again. Right at his heart, which felt like a fist beating against his ribs.

Hazard said, "Come here again asking for meds without cash in hand, and you will limp out of here leaving a trail of blood. Do you understand me?"

Zach swallowed hard and it hurt and he hated the sound of it, hated the way Hazard's head tilted when it happened. Zach dropped his eyes and nodded.

The gun waved at the door.

"Get out," Hazard said.

8

Zach made it past the basketball court, ignoring the kids out there who stared at him, before the fear gave way to anger. His hands shook, so he clenched and unclenched his fists until the skin of his palms burned. A ray of sunlight came through a hole in the clouds and shone off a pile of snow. It made his eyes ache.

Who the fuck was Hazard to pull a gun on him just because he asked for a favor? Hazard, an obsessive-compulsive drug dealer, someone he'd given how much money to, and the asshole points a gun at him?

Zach didn't think Hazard would've killed him.

Shot him, yes. But not killed him. He'd have shot Zach right through the shoulder, or the leg, then dragged him screaming down the hall and dumped him on the stairs... or maybe in the empty pool with all the other discarded objects.

He thought Hazard had been cool, eccentric maybe—a little high strung, but cool. Maybe even a friend, or something close to one. But it turned out he was no different than everyone else who had something you needed, and kept it from you. The government, corporations, colleges. If you had money you were all right. If you were poor, fuck you.

Zach slammed a closed fist into an open palm and the pain shot through his bones. Deep down he knew though, fair was fair. You didn't get something for nothing.

The hole in the clouds closed up and the world went gray as Zach turned onto a street he knew would eventually lead him downtown. He didn't know what he'd do once he got there, but he'd figure something out.

Downtown, where the hospital was. The place Mom worked. The place where Dad's body had been stored in a freezer until the funeral home picked him up.

In his mind, Zach saw the hospital, saw the long

sterile hallways. Saw Mom mopping the floors with disinfectant, the stuff she always smelled like when she came home. And Zach couldn't think of Mom without thinking of Tessa. Maybe the morphine was starting to wear off, but all these images were so clear and he saw his sister's face, remembered hearing her cry through the wall of his bedroom in the weeks after Dad died. Why hadn't he ever gone to her, comforted her? Because he had nothing to give, or at least that's what he told himself. But Tessa had the same pain, so did Mom, and Zach was only making things worse for both of them by following Dad into the dark.

Maybe not having the money, and having nothing left to sell, was a sign for him to finally stop. Stop taking the pills. Stop living in a hazy world of numbness. Maybe this was exactly what he needed. Just go cold, let the shakes hit, the shits, whatever came with it. Besides, all that hurt he was trying to bury, it wasn't staying buried anymore. Like seeing Mom this morning—it hurt that he hurt her. It hurt that he failed her, and this pain was new. It wasn't the pain of losing Dad, it was the pain of everything that came after. Hurt on top of hurt. Maybe he just needed to feel all of it.

93

Zach actually smiled a little at the thought of being done with the pills. He'd apologize to his mom and Tessa, ask for forgiveness. His eyes burned at the thought of hugging his mom and telling her he'd do better, be better. And that was what he really wanted more than anything. He longed to wake up and face a day in which he wasn't ashamed of every moment of his existence.

Every pill was a failure.

Every failure severed something inside him.

And every cut left vital pieces of himself in tatters.

He wanted all those pieces sewn back together into a better, stronger version of himself.

This was it. He was done. Done with the pills, the numbing himself to pain. In fact, he'd start right now by going back home and cleaning the entire house. He'd make a meal for Mom to eat when she woke up, maybe even pack her a lunch for at work.

He smiled again and it was like a weight lifted off his chest. He breathed deep and felt the air go deeper than it had in months.

Zach was about to turn around and head back the way he'd come when a cold breeze blew through the fabric of his sweatshirt and chilled the sweat on his back.

He shivered and noticed a flash of color from a yard up ahead. Red, bright against the snow, standing in the lawn with nothing else around it. The muscles in Zach's chest spasmed a little. He had to get closer.

What it looked like was impossible, because no one would leave something like that sitting outside, especially not in a neighborhood like this. Zach scanned the street, the houses, for any movement, any people walking or trimming trees. But the street was quiet and still. Not as unnaturally quiet as the other street had been—there was a sense of this place moving at normal speed—but enough so that even his footsteps seemed loud.

Zach approached slowly and watched the windows of the house. The curtains were white and drawn, and there were no shapes moving on the other side. He rubbed his fingers against his palms.

Soon he was standing right at the edge of the lawn. Empty driveway, silent home with faded blue siding. He waited and listened. The breeze rattled branches together above his head.

He was close enough to see that the curved metal was exactly what he thought it was. But no, not exactly. Better somehow, even though he wasn't sure how.

Standing in the snow, propped up on its kickstand, was a shining bicycle—vintage, straight out of one of Hazard's movies. Whitewall tires so clean and black they looked like they'd never even been on the road, and the frame sparkled with paint the color of fresh blood.

And as he looked at the bike a hunger grew in Zach, a desire so strong his body went weak. Thoughts of Mom and Tessa faded until they were like the chalk outline of a body on the street after it had rained. He imagined the bitter taste of morphine dissolving on his tongue, the soft explosion in his head when the medication hit.

More than anything in the world he wanted the pills, and this bike was how he'd get them.

9

Zach Ayers heard a hum coming from somewhere. A low, metallic vibration that made his eyes feel like they were shaking. A constant throbbing sound, faint but unmistakable. He looked down the street, then in the other direction, but couldn't see anything that might be causing the noise.

He blinked hard a few times and took a step from the sidewalk into the yard, and there was no question now. It was the bike. The metal frame hummed like a voice and Zach felt almost the same as he had when that cop stared at him, like his thoughts were seen, somehow. This sound found hidden thoughts and clarified them, pulled them forward, made sense of them. Flashes of his dad, his mom, his sister, his future—they appeared and disappeared with each transition in the pitch of the hum. It was singing all his fears into shapes.

Zach came closer. Close enough to reach out and touch the handlebars. The snow underneath the tires was melted, showing green, wet grass. The whitewall tires didn't have a speck of dirt on them, and the leather saddle shined like brand new. It was like someone had just pulled the bike out of a garage where it had sat for sixty years, untouched, unridden.

The frame looked like an old cantilevered Schwinn Monark from the fifties, with the thick tank and carrier behind the saddle, but the handlebars and chain guard looked more like the ones Ghost made in the late seventies.

A custom job then, Zach thought, circling around the bike.

He ran his fingers along the metal frame, a dark red the same color as the liquid that filled the vial when he had his blood drawn at the doctor's office, and the hum moved through his skin, vibrated the beads of sweat on his arm. A small black flag hung from a thin pole on the back, a coiled snake at its center. Something was off about the frame, though, but he couldn't figure it out.

Custom for sure. Whoever made it probably combined a few classic designs into something completely unique. Zach guessed the bike would probably cost close to two grand new, so he figured he could get an easy seven hundred for it from Mike, the chubby mechanic downtown who bought whatever Zach stole.

A strange shimmer grew in the air around the bike as he touched it, like the fumes above an open can of gasoline, and the hum grew louder—a steady, rhythmic pulse that throbbed in his chest. The red frame became a blur, all the metal and chrome vibrating with the hum. It wasn't unpleasant, but it made him uneasy.

He looked up at the house. Curtains and blinds covered all the windows, and there was no light coming from between the cracks. If anyone lived there they were either asleep, or more likely, as high as birds.

Pain stabbed his side as he thought about taking the bike—actually, he more than thought about it. He imagined it, watched it play out on the movie screen of his mind. But that guilt kept digging into him, making him double over in agony. He never broke into houses or cars, never took anything that was secured or locked down, and he told himself that counted for something in a world whose teeth were forever ripping things away from him.

Zach looked at the house again, and then, with his heart slamming away in his chest, he grabbed the handlebars. All at once the pain in his side went away. The vibrations moved through the metal and into his hands. And it felt good, better than good.

He lifted the kickstand with his heel and rolled the bike through the snow, out of the lawn.

He glanced back and saw a shadow flutter on the living room curtains. Just a flash of a figure, then it was gone. It reappeared on the curtains of the upstairs bedroom, a dark figure with an elongated torso and long spindly arms. The image flickered again, onto the curtains of what Zach thought was probably the kitchen, and lingered there, watching him. The head twisted against the fabric, following Zach as he left the grass. A head the same shape as the cop's.

He couldn't understand what was happening—was it one person, or several, popping up in rooms all over the house? Or maybe it was a projection, some elaborate Halloween-type prank. Then the figure lifted a hand and pressed it against the fabric. The fingers raked along the curtain, closing into a fist. Cold wrapped around Zach's chest and he struggled to take a breath.

He pushed faster, and as soon as he hit the sidewalk Zach put his feet on the pedals and started pumping. The moment the chain caught and started spinning the wheels, the vibration spread over the palms of his hands and moved up his arms. At first, he thought it was just friction, but as he sped down the street the vibration grew until his skin began to sting. He looked over his shoulder and the house was already out of view, but a car had just rounded the corner one block down, so he pedaled even harder.

He took a quick glance backward and leaned, planning to hang a right at the next block, but when he saw the dark blue and white colors of the car, when he heard something like rat claws scratching through his thoughts, he lost his concentration and almost missed the turn.

The bike turned anyway. The handlebars moved smoothly, even though he hadn't moved them, and took him onto a new street, speeding farther into the neighborhood.

His hands shook as the vibration grew stronger, and with it came heat. It reminded him of when he and some friends went down to the depot and grabbed onto the tracks, feeling the tremors of an approaching train. Those long pieces of metal singing with the mass and velocity of something still so far off they couldn't see it. And now, the handlebars thrumming made his bones feel like they were melting.

The street was empty, so Zach stopped pedaling and coasted past a few rundown houses. He went to lift his right hand, shake it out a little, but the fingers wouldn't budge from the handlebar. He tried again, harder, thinking maybe the owner wanted someone to steal the bike, and put superglue on the grips to punish the thief.

Sweat slid down the skin of his back, snaked into his boxers. It itched a line down the sides of his face and he tried to lift his hand to wipe it away, but the hand wouldn't move, not even a little bit. He tried the left hand—same thing. All the muscles and tendons started to cramp up, making him grip the handlebars tighter. Zach thought of the electric fence he had grabbed when he was a kid, and how he couldn't let go as the current traveled through him.

Zach's heart fell out of rhythm. At first, the adrenaline of stealing the bike caused his heart to beat faster, a rush of excitement and fear, now it was a galloping horse tripping over its own legs, and every time his heart skipped a beat Zach felt a pocket of air move up his throat.

Zach knew there was an explanation for why his hands couldn't let go of the handlebars, but his mind couldn't find it. He still wasn't scared, not yet. That came when he moved to kick his right leg out and his foot stayed where it was, spinning the pedal around and around.

There were no brake levers on the handlebars, so Zach tried to slam the pedals backward but his legs kept pumping like pistons.

The quick raspy breaths that didn't seem to reach his lungs—Zach told himself it was because he was riding, but some part of his brain knew better.

Something is wrong with the bike.

Zach shoved this thought as deep as it would go, and told himself that the fight or flight instinct was keeping him glued to the bike. His own subconscious wouldn't let him off until he was out of harm's way.

The vibrations spread into his shoulders and neck, and when Zach looked down at the bloody red frame, it seemed brighter than before. The paint pulsed with light, like an ember in a fire pit. A heart beating inside the metal.

Then he became aware of his legs—they were moving on the pedals, but he wasn't making any effort to push. There had to be something inside the bike, some kind of hidden engine that propelled the thing, kept it upright. It was moving the pedals all by itself—Zach's feet just happened to be attached to them.

He tried to move the handlebars, to the turn the bike left or right, and the tire didn't move at all.

But I steered it once, Zach thought. *I turned onto this street.*

Unless… he hadn't actually steered it.

He pulled and yanked, and the bike kept tearing a straight path down the center of the road.

The thought came clawing back up to the surface, pushing aside every rational idea until it was all he could think.

Something is definitely fucking wrong with the bike.

Zach Ayers clenched his eyes as tight as he could. An inner voice screamed that whatever he thought was happening was impossible. But that voice was drowned out by another, louder, voice. This voice kept saying, *possible doesn't matter right now. You are on a bike that is hauling ass all by itself. And let's not forget the shadow.*

Shit, Zach thought, opening his eyes. *The shadow.*

Something in his brain popped, and it made

him think of a black balloon filled with absolute terror. Somehow he had been protecting this fragile bubble, and as soon as he thought of the shadow it burst, spilling all that fear, like a dark liquid flooding his mind. A metallic taste filled his mouth, the taste of a dentist's instrument after it has drawn blood.

The bike tore through a small pile of dead leaves on the sidewalk, brown and wet, the leaves stuck to the tires and were flung off like flat, dead animals. Everywhere Zach looked was deserted, as if the people on this street knew to stay indoors, knew to stay away from the bike.

He tried to calm his panicked breathing and think about the situation rationally.

"It's just a bike," he said, out loud.

Hearing the fear in his voice only made it more real inside him.

"It's just a fucking bike!" he shouted, and pulled his hands as hard as he could, trying to lift the front tire into the air. It didn't budge from the road.

It had to be superglue. The handlebars must have been covered in the stuff. Every inch of his skin was stuck, and no matter how hard he pulled the skin didn't lift up off the rubber at all. Zach didn't care if he tore off all his skin, he just wanted off the bike. He clenched his teeth and tried again, this time pulling his arms so hard that his elbow joints popped.

"Shit."

His lungs burned now, and he hated the feeling of being trapped, being tied down to something with invisible wires. It reminded him of when Brett Calvert's older brother, Reggie, had held him underwater at the public pool. Zach thrashed and fought to escape Reggie's grip, but he was too big, too strong, and Zach was so certain his mouth would open in a scream and water would come rushing into his lungs that he almost blacked out.

That memory made even more sweat drip down Zach's face. He wanted to wipe it away, stop it from getting into his eyes, but he couldn't. He tried his best to rub his face into his shoulder, but he couldn't quite get all of the sweat, and some of it slid into his eyes and stung.

He thrashed, just like he had when Reggie held him under. He started screaming. His arms shook as he pushed and pulled, like the bike was something he was trying to strangle. Still, his hands and feet stayed where they were, melted to the handlebars and pedals like Zach was part of the bike now.

He jerked his arms back and forth to turn, and the bike still kept going straight. Houses went by in a blur. An old woman in a bathrobe came out of one and picked up the newspaper. Zach barely saw her face break into a smile, saw her hand lift in a wave, before she was behind him, shrinking in the distance.

Zach screamed, "Help me," but the old woman was already going back inside.

10

The bike kept a steady pace down the center of the road. Zach thought it strange that something that seemed so sentient should be so silent. He would expect it to growl like an animal as it ate up the asphalt, or hiss like the snake on the black flag that snapped in the wind.

But the bike sounded just like any other bike. The drone of the tires on the road, the faint click of the pedals as they turned. And Zach's heavy breathing.

His hands started to cramp up, so Zach loosened his grip as much as he could and relaxed his arms. He looked down at the gleaming red frame and saw half his face reflected on the surface.

Zach leaned closer to the pulsing metal and whispered, "Hello?"

He didn't expect a reply, and he didn't get one.

"What's the plan here?" Zach said.

The tires kept rolling and the pedals kept turning.

Zach straightened and pointed his face at the sky. He closed his eyes and took a breath.

"Someone has to be driving this thing, right? Remote control or something. I bet there's a camera somewhere, a microphone maybe?"

He looked back down at the bike, listened for the whir of a tiny machine hidden somewhere he couldn't see it. He heard nothing but the tires and the pedals.

"So, whoever you are, if you can hear me, I'm sorry. I never should have taken the bike. I know it was wrong but I did it anyway. I could tell you the whole story but I don't think it'd matter all that much. I fucked up, and I'm sorry."

Zach closed his eyes again as they burned with tears. He saw Mom's face, staring at him in the kitchen, her hands covered in soap bubbles. As if she didn't clean enough already, there she was, cleaning up the mess he'd made.

"Please just let me get off," Zach said. "I'll pay you for any scratches or dings."

Up ahead a truck came onto the street, driving toward Zach. His fingers gripped the handlebars tighter.

"Listen, man, I saw your house is kind of beat up, in need of a paint job."

There were cars parked on either side of the street, and if the bike didn't move he'd run straight into the truck that was coming closer by the second. Through the dirty windshield he could see the face of the man driving, baseball cap pulled down low, and his eyes looked confused, maybe even angry, that Zach hadn't moved out of the way.

"I'm not a bad painter," Zach said, and he hated the fear that crept into his voice. The breathless words sounded like pleading.

"I could pay for the paint and then do the job for free."

The guy in the truck honked the horn and the sound was so loud and so unexpected that Zach's whole body jerked.

"I know what to do," Zach said, almost yelling now. "I'll sand it down, use some primer. I'll even do the trim."

The truck was so close Zach saw the faded black hat and red letter "B" logo of the Boston Red Sox. The man's eyes were narrowed, his mouth tight. He laid into the horn and kept it pushed as he came barreling down the center of the street, and the obnoxious blare made Zach realize—

The guy wasn't going to move.

He was the truck, Zach was nothing but a bike. This guy would run over him like a speedbump made of flesh and metal.

Zach screamed as loud as he could, "I can't stop! I can't stop!"

Maybe if the horn hadn't been blasting the guy would have heard him, but with that noise filling Zach's head he knew there was no way the driver understood.

The grille of the truck looked like the mouth of some metal monster, the unlit headlights dead eyes. A machine, being controlled the same as the machine Zach was stuck to. Maybe the guy had stolen that truck, and as soon as he started driving his hands melted to the steering wheel. Maybe his foot was stuck pressing down on the gas pedal.

Is this how the ride ends? Zach thought.

Up until now, there hadn't been time to really think about what would happen an hour, two hours, twelve hours from now.

Zach looked at the driver—the truck so close he could hear the roar of the engine, the squeal of an old belt—and the man's eyes were so big the pupils were just black circles in a pools of white.

Zach closed his eyes, waited for the impact, and hoped it wouldn't hurt too bad before he stopped breathing.

Time slipped, broke down.

The driver was yelling something but his mouth moved in slow motion. Snow flurries, kicked up by the bike's tires, floated gently through the air, hovering like seeds blown from a dandelion. Zach had heard that a person's life played out in front of their eyes, like a movie on fast forward, right before they died. But Zach didn't see his whole life—all he saw was the last twenty-four hours. The buried hurt in Tessa's face. The disappointment, and love so raw it was angry, etched into every wrinkle around his mom's eyes.

I exist and cause pain, Zach thought. *I hurt and cause hurt.*

When the drugs wore off, when feeling sparked to

life under the numbness, that was when the emptiness and loneliness covered him like a cold blanket. And he hated every miserable second of feeling that way. But even then, he loved his mom and his sister. He wanted to see Tessa become whatever she was going to be. He wanted to see the weight somehow get lifted off Mom's shoulders, see her full of joy again.

And all those things were in the future… so he'd have to be in the future to see them.

He wanted to be alive. All the pain, all the loss, all the joy, and all the love.

Zach opened his eyes and time caught up, and the truck was close enough that Zach could have reached out and touched it, if he could lift his hands. The driver's mouth was open so wide Zach could see the fillings in the man's teeth.

On instinct, Zach jerked the handlebars to the right, and to his surprise they turned and the bike veered between two parked cars, bounced over the curb, and skidded onto the sidewalk. Not once did it stop moving.

The truck screeched to a stop. Zach turned his head and saw the driver get out, hunch over, and put both hands on his knees like he was going to throw up.

The bike sped past four houses, then shot off the curb and back onto the street. Zach felt the discs in his spine compress with the shuddering bounce.

They tore down the street, faster now. Zach could feel it in the way the air blew colder over his face, the way his legs pumped. He smiled a little, because now he knew something he hadn't known before.

He had turned the handlebars to move out of the way of the truck.

He could control the bike.

11

A feeling that Zach could only think of as joy washed over him. Clear and purified, it electrified his skin, made him actually start pushing the pedals himself. The clarity of the feeling was unusual, but familiar. It was something he'd felt a long time ago, a feeling he wanted to get back ever since Dad died.

Zach decided to test the limits of his control. He moved the handlebars to the left and right. The front tire followed his motion and he yelled out in triumph. He weaved the bike down the street, back and forth in long

S-shaped patterns.

The air, sharp and clean, burned his nostrils and filled his lungs. He saw the houses, the cars, the trees, and snow in vivid detail. He felt like he was speeding down a hyperreal street in a hallucination brought on by the best high he'd ever experienced.

But he wasn't high, and he knew that now. All the adrenaline and motion must have burned the morphine out of his system. He wasn't numb anymore.

He yelled again, a war whoop so loud it made his throat raw.

Zach took the bike from one side of the street to the other. He still couldn't pull his hands away, and there was still no way to brake, but for now, knowing he could steer the fucking thing was enough for him.

"All right, you son of a bitch," he said, smiling. "Deal's off. The bike is coming back, and if you don't bring something to dissolve the superglue on my hands, I'm busting this thing to pieces right on the sidewalk."

He saw an open driveway up ahead without any cars parked in it and thought that was the perfect place to do a one-eighty, start speeding in the other direction. He'd have to be careful though, because he wouldn't be able to slow down before he made the turn. And was it just his imagination, or was the bike going a little faster than before? Not much, but enough to feel the sting of the air coming off the snow just a little more.

Zach moved to the right, planning to make a wide left turn into the driveway. It would have to be close to avoid the cars parked along the street. But if he cut it tight, he could make it.

He waited until he was just past the driveway, then he wrenched the wheel to the left. The tires scraped asphalt and threw a spray of slushy snow onto the parked car. The bike hit the driveway at full speed, and Zach kept the handlebars turned so far his muscles cramped with the effort.

The bike came out of the driveway, and Zach leaned away as the edge of the handlebars scraped a line into the faded paint of a brown Dodge Dart. He whooped again, and if he could have moved his hands he would have been pumping his fists into the air.

Now he faced the other direction, looking back down the long, shadowed street.

All he wanted was to get the bike back to the owner. He'd get on his knees and beg for forgiveness, if that was what this guy wanted. Anything to be done with this whole thing and let it become just a hazy memory. One of those stories you tell years later when all the fear has drained out of the events.

The bike sped past two houses and then came to a sudden and complete stop.

There was no screech of tires burning the road. The brakes didn't engage, at least not that Zach was aware of, but the bike went from full motion to complete stop so fast Zach's whole body was thrown forward. His head snapped back so hard he heard a loud *pop* and his eyes went fuzzy.

He waited for the ground to come rushing up, slam into the side of his face. It would hurt like hell because he couldn't do a thing to stop the fall. He clenched his eyes tight and braced for an impact—

That never came.

His eyes opened slowly and he saw trees reaching up into the sky. Nothing was upside down or sideways. The bike stood upright, Zach's feet still stuck to the pedals.

Zach's arms quivered. He felt the muscles in his throat shaking. He sat on a bike that was defying physics. If time had slowed down before when the truck was coming at him, it had completely frozen now.

There was no way a bike could stand on two tires without toppling over. Whatever liquid was left in that black balloon, the rest spilled out and covered all his thoughts until they were dripping with dark matter.

He was wrong. So, so wrong.

There was no machine controlling this thing. And he had known that all along, hadn't he? He just didn't want to admit it. Anything powerful enough to propel and steer this bike would be visible, and noisy. There was nothing. And whatever kept his hands and feet pinned, if it was glue he'd be able to rip his skin right off. But he couldn't. Because it wasn't glue. It was something he didn't have a name for, and that made a chill crawl down his back like an icy finger tracing his spine.

Zach was about to say something, anything, but he could no longer pretend there was some weird guy back at that house with a remote control and camera, making this bike do what it did. Zach bit down on his lip until his eyes watered. If he *could* find the words, Zach didn't know who he'd be talking to. And that scared him more than anything.

Then, very slowly, the bike began to turn in place,

as if on a platform. The tires scraped the ground and Zach faced the parked cars, now the houses, the trees, and finally the street again. Back the way they'd been going before.

"Oh, shit," Zach said. "Shit, shit, shit."

The words had barely left his mouth before the bike took off, like an arrow shot from a bow. The sudden acceleration pulled Zach's head back, and he had to fight to keep looking straight ahead. The wind whipped at his face, made his eyes go dry.

Faster. Faster.

So much faster than it had gone before. And that's when Zach knew—

This bike has a destination.

12

Zach Ayers wasn't about to give up so easy. No matter what propelled this thing, it was just a bike, after all. How much stronger could it be than the human riding it?

Cars whipped by. Heat bloomed in Zach's knees as his legs pedaled faster and faster. Tears streamed from his eyes. Wherever the bike was taking him, he didn't want to go. The fear, that cold black liquid, covered all his thoughts now. The bike was punishment, that much was clear. But for what, he didn't know.

For becoming an addict, just like Dad?

For putting his mom and Tessa through the same

thing Dad had put them all through?

What did it matter? He was guilty of all of it. Maybe he deserved the punishment, if that was what it was, but he sure as hell didn't want it.

He yanked the handlebars to the right, and the bike yanked them back so fast Zach's wrist popped. He hissed and tried pulling to the left. Again, the bike moved the tire straight with a strong motion he couldn't stop from happening. Something within the metal itself fought against his hands and righted the bike. It was like struggling against a ghost.

His sweatshirt was soaked with sweat under the arms, around the neck. Cold air blew through the wet fabric and chilled his skin.

The bike wasn't going to let him make another big turn like the last one. If Zach wouldn't play along, this blood-red bike would keep him going straight.

But straight to where?

Zach's body started to ache with fatigue. His legs didn't want to keep moving, and his hands didn't want to grip. He'd give anything to be home right now, lying in his bed listening to music, just knowing that his mom and sister were in the house. Safe.

"I don't want to go wherever you're taking me," Zach said, hoping that whatever intelligence was present inside all the metal and chrome could understand him. "I want to go home."

He gently moved the handlebars to the left. The bike let him slowly veer toward an open driveway, then it just as gently veered back to the center of the road.

Zach tried not to cry, but he couldn't help it.

"I want to go home," he said again. "Please, just let me go. I swear to God I'll never steal another bike as long as I live."

He waited as they sailed through an intersection, through a four-way stop. Snow drifted down between tree branches, touched Zach's warm cheeks with a cold kiss. He waited as more cars and houses flew by. He could almost imagine that the background was moving around him, and he was at a standstill on the strange bike.

"Give me an answer," Zach said finally.

The snow fell heavier, thick flakes that swirled like a tunnel around him as they sped through it.

The bike rode, silent and steady.

Zach decided he didn't care what happened to him. Clearly, he was never going to leave this bike until it arrived wherever it wanted to go. All Zach knew was that he couldn't ride another minute without fighting the thing with everything he had.

"Give me a fucking answer!" Zach screamed. He straightened both arms and twisted to the left as hard as he could. The bike let him steer for just a couple of seconds before taking control again, then the front tire wrenched to the right and went full speed toward a parked car. Just before it was about to crash, the bike turned again and slammed Zach's leg into the body of the car.

Something snapped, something deep in the flesh, and a searing electric pain shot up the leg into Zach's hip. He screamed as the bike dragged him down the car. He felt another snap in his ribs, this one even sharper, as the side-view mirror collided with his chest.

The broken leg kept pedaling and every revolution made Zach's head lighter and lighter. Another car came into view, and Zach barely had time to yell out before the knee of his bad leg shattered the rear headlight.

He vomited hot acid all over his sweatshirt.

He looked down at his leg and saw shredded jeans, pieces of red-tinted glass embedded in the flesh. Warm liquid ran down his shin, into his shoes. The pain was unlike anything Zach had ever experienced. Just when he thought it couldn't get any worse, the pedal would turn and he would howl with agony. Over and over again.

Worst of all, he couldn't escape it. It made him think of those videos everyone had seen, the ones taken in a bare room in some other country. People thought to have information, tied down and tortured until they said whatever the torturer wanted to hear.

You'd say, do, anything just to make the pain stop.

"Stop," Zach said. "Please stop."

Zach's whole body went into tremors. The muscles in his legs shivered like he'd been swimming in a pool in the middle of winter. His teeth chattered so hard he was afraid they might break.

His vision grew blurry as the bike came close to another car, this time aiming so that Zach's knuckles clipped the side-view mirror. He screamed out, "God damn it!" The mirror broke off the car and went skittering across the street. Blood poured from Zach's hand, trailed along the handlebars. He could see shiny white bone poking out from the torn-up flesh.

"I can't take any more," Zach said, out of breath. "Please, no more."

And the leg kept turning, and each new bolt of pain made more acid burn up his throat. The world went hazy, like it did when the morphine hit, but this was so much worse.

"Please…"

He lifted his head just in time to see a low-hanging tree branch coming straight at his face. He closed his eyes and the wood cracked his skull. An explosion of white light burst inside his head. The sound of rushing water filled his ears. Warmth spread down his back.

And Zach Ayers's memory stopped recording.

13

Zach was alone in a cold dark room. Wind blew at his face, bit his skin. His skeleton glowed red hot inside him. Gravity had switched off and he was weightless, floating in black space. On the wall in front of him—at least he thought it must have been a wall—there were two curved white lines spaced a few feet apart.

Maybe they were windows, strange-shaped windows. He tried to swim, to move his arms and legs against the air. He floated closer and the shapes on the wall changed as he neared them. They seemed to be opening wider and wider until they were two large ovals, big enough to swim through.

They *were* windows, and he could see out now. A street, houses, trees, cars, and snow. All rushing past.

His hands bumped into the black wall and he hovered there, just at the oval windows. Zach put his face to the glass and looked out. He saw two hands, one all torn up and bloody, on the handlebars of a bike. He looked down and saw two feet on the pedals. Feet wearing shoes exactly like the ones he was wearing.

Zach yelled and pushed himself away from the windows.

Those were his eyes. He was looking out through his own face.

He floated backward, expecting to hit another wall at any moment, but that moment never came. He just kept going further into the dark, and the windows of his eyes grew smaller and smaller until they disappeared.

14

Simon Tanner didn't want to play outside—he was ten levels deep into *The Bone Dungeon*—but after lunch his mother made him put on his snowsuit and go out into the cold. He complained the whole time she helped guide his arms into the puffy sleeves, shoved a wool hat down over his ears, until she finally grounded him from the video game for the rest of the week.

Simon stomped into the front yard and said every curse word he knew, even threw in a few *butt-faces* and *barf-eaters* because he knew how mad it would make Mom if she could hear him, and kicked snow until he didn't even feel the cold anymore.

The street was quiet and snow fell so thick he couldn't even see all the way to the end of the block. He plopped down in the yard and sat there, looking up at the millions of snowflakes as they drifted down out of the sky.

His mitten-covered hand brushed the thick powder, and he thought about building a snowman. How long had it been? Years, maybe. Simon was only nine years old and he already felt that building a humanoid shape out of frozen water was a baby thing to do.

But as he sat there, Simon couldn't stop thinking about how fun it would be to create a monster snowman. Not one of those cheerful smiling ones, but a fearsome creature to guard his home from intruders. He would give it two heads instead of one, and each face would contain a mouthful of razor-sharp teeth. Its eyes would be red instead of black, and it would have long claws.

Simon smiled. Yes, that was exactly what he'd do. If he couldn't play *The Bone Dungeo*n, he'd create his own.

He had just finished rolling the first ball, the foundation for the rest of his monster, when he saw a flash of red inside the swirling white snow far down the street. A bike came into view and it was moving fast, way faster than any other bike he'd seen on their street. He wasn't sure how he knew that, but there was something about the way it moved. Something... different.

The bike sped onto Simon's block, and the rider's head didn't move to look both ways before crossing the dangerous intersection Simon's mother always warned him about. And it was the rider that confused Simon the most. A teenager, it looked like, definitely not dressed for the weather. The rider's legs moved the pedals, but his head hung limply, like he was asleep. He didn't look up or watch where he was going. In fact, his whole upper body was slouched too.

The bike was just three houses away now. Simon swallowed hard. The rider looked dead, and was that blood all over his leg? It had to be. The pants were ripped apart and he saw angry red flesh underneath, all raw and shredded like the Green Knights after they got trapped in Mortok the Executioner's lair.

Simon Tanner forgot all about his snowman monster and stood up, a fistful of snow falling from his hand. How could that guy still be riding if he was dead?

Simon was sure something was wrong with the bike. It was blurry for one thing, and at first Simon thought that must be his eyesight. He'd been having trouble seeing what the teacher wrote on the whiteboard lately. But it wasn't his eyes. The red frame of the bike was mesmerizing, and like the fire his dad built when they went camping, it pulsed.

Simon blinked a few times and the bike sped past him with a sound like Mom zipping up his puffy coat. The rider was either sleeping or dead, there was no other option. Unless—

Unless the rider had known a kid would be outside building a snowman and he was just playing a trick. But how could he have known?

Simon wasn't cold anymore because he'd started sweating, and a chill went up his neck as he watched the rider pass by. The whole side of his face was dark red with blood. His sweatshirt was stained with it.

And still, he kept riding. His limp body moving the pedals and riding the bike so fast it was gone from view before Simon could even manage a single word. And by the time Simon found his voice, that single word was "shit."

15

The dark room grew brighter. Zach's body slowed down and eventually came to a stop. Without kicking, or waving his arms, his body was thrown back toward the windows. He flew faster and faster, and those strange windows grew so big he was afraid he'd go crashing right through them.

The outside world filled his vision and he held up his hands to protect his face.

Then—

His eyes fluttered open. Pain hammered a straight line from his leg to his brain. He blinked a few times, looked down at his hands on the white grips, his legs moving without his permission. He opened his mouth and felt something stretch and crack, around his lips, his chin.

The wind hit colder on half his forehead, and it burned. He lifted his eyebrows and felt skin separate, opening and closing like a second mouth. Whenever he did, a fresh rush of blood ran down around his eye.

His heartbeat was like the bass in one of those souped-up racers with the subwoofer pounding. With each revolution of the pedals, the broken bones in his leg shifted, scraped together. The muscles in his thigh were going numb.

What he wouldn't give for some morphine, right now. Wrap that pain in some chemical gauze and suffocate it.

"Let me off," Zach pleaded. "I'm begging you, just make this stop."

As if hearing his voice, the pedals stopped turning and the bike coasted as it came to another intersection. They had slowed down enough for Zach to read the street sign just as the bike took a sharp left onto Archer Way.

"No!" Zach yelled.

The pedals turned again and the bike picked up

speed. Zach almost didn't feel the bone-scraping pain anymore. All he could hear was his own breathing, filling his ears like the ocean waves on Mom's sound machine.

"Not this street," Zach said, "any street but this one."

The bike rode straight down the center of the road, narrowly avoiding a car that passed by. The driver, young, wearing a gold chain, held up his middle finger at Zach.

Zach tried pulling up on his hands to lift the handlebars, but the front tire didn't leave the road. It was as glued to the asphalt as Zach's hands were to the rubber grips.

"Why won't you listen to me?" Zach asked.

He couldn't go any farther down this street, couldn't stand to see that gray house again, and if that meant purposefully crashing he was willing to do it. Zach threw his whole upper body to the side, then to the other side, trying to knock the bike over. It didn't move.

He wondered what he looked like to the people he'd seen. Did something appear strange, or did he just look like a frantic young man riding somewhere as if his life depended on it? Zach's heart sank a little to think that most of them probably thought he was on his way to score drugs. Where else would someone wide-eyed and sweaty, covered in cuts, bruises, and blood be going in such a hurry?

What they couldn't see, couldn't know, was that Zach had no control over his actions.

A possession from the outside in.

Oh God, this street. A place he saw in his worst dreams. In fact, a place he visited almost every single night. He knew how far ahead the house was, could see the twisted tree out front. The one that was burned black from when lightning had struck it during a freak summer storm.

The gray two-story came into view. It looked exactly like it did in his nightmares, except in his dreams he was never afraid of the house. But now, seeing it loom in the distance, his forehead broke out in sweat that dripped into the open cut and stung. His heart skipped beats.

The house wasn't just some location in a dreamscape. It was here, it was real, and it seemed to expand and contract, as if it were breathing. Something Zach knew couldn't be true. Maybe it was just his vision, but the sagging roof looked like it filled more of the sky than it had before. Those pillars, weather beaten and scarred, made it look like the front of the house was hunched down, like a gorilla, ready to come pounding into the street and crush him.

Vines curled around the pillars like green veins, and the front door still didn't match the rest of the house. It was wood colored, solid, no windows. The original house must have had a white door with windows, but whoever lived there now had removed it. Or, more likely, the cops had kicked it in at some point, and this was the replacement.

The bike came to a full stop directly in front of the house, once again ignoring physics and staying upright on its two tires. Zach was momentarily grateful for the rest it gave his bad leg, but he would rather be anywhere else on earth than here.

The bike, in the center of the street, faced straight ahead, so Zach had to turn his head to look at the house. It had been pure gray once, but now it was the color of a sweat-stained T-shirt, storm splattered with mud from the overflowing gutters. Tall weeds covered the lawn, the dark vines that twisted up around the pillars curled under the shingles on the roof. Black mold grew along the siding in ominous patterns. Half the bricks had fallen off the chimney and lay scattered around the lawn like small rust-colored gravestones.

He sat there, fused to a bike that defied gravity, balanced on its two wheels, and he couldn't stop looking at the circle in front of the house where the asphalt was a darker shade of black.

Motion up ahead turned his attention away from the place where his father had died, and he looked farther down the street as a blue and white car turned onto Archer.

Zach didn't even have to see the driver to know who was behind the wheel. The way his thoughts turned to smoke and felt rummaged through, like thin claws were digging through the mist of his innermost feelings, told him all he needed to know.

Zach sensed something behind him and turned to see another blue and white car on the street behind him. The light bar on top flashed red and white, and the siren gave off two *whoop-whoops*.

He leaned down to the bike.

"Wherever we're going, now would be a good time to speed up and get there fast."

The bike stayed upright, unmoving.

"Go!" Zach screamed. "Get me out of here."

The cop car in front crawled toward him, those dark glasses staring at him through the windshield. Zach looked behind him and the other car was coming closer too.

And the gray house loomed over him, still and silent. The dark porch and curtained windows like a mouth and eyes drawn on a painted face.

16

All the pain in Zach's body disappeared as he stared, not at the house, but at that dark misshapen circle on the road. Time seemed to run backward. All the sounds of the world, his own body, slipped into silence. His mind located a memory, pulled it up, and projected it onto the scene before him. A faint afterimage of something he could never forget, no matter how hard he tried. Dad's body on the ground, curled in a fetal position, skin black and hardened and cracked, and those cracks were bright red lines that showed the flesh underneath. Thin strands of smoke rose from the motionless body, and Zach couldn't recognize his dad, couldn't know it was him. But he knew. The size and shape of the body, the way it was curled up. The burnt rubber soles of his shoes, the gold band of his wedding ring bright against the black skin, and a small piece of blue fabric on the street, burned at the edges. The shirt Dad had been wearing when he left the house.

The cop cars crept closer, the silent lights of the one behind him casting carnival colors as the sky grew darker.

The memory faded but Zach still stared at the place where his dad had died, his eyes blurry with tears.

"Why did you bring me here?" he asked the bike.

The bike didn't move, but the frame began to vibrate and it reminded him of lying on one of those coin-operated beds in the cheap motels they had lived in for weeks at a time when he was just a kid.

He tried to fight the tears, but he couldn't stop them from coming. "The one place I never wanted to see again, and this is where you bring me?"

The chain rattled as the metal around it quivered. He felt the broken bone in his leg shift with the pulse of the bike.

"I didn't want to be like this," Zach said, as tears

ran freely. "I just didn't want to hurt anymore."

He bent his left leg and pushed his foot down as hard as he could, trying to snap the pedal off.

Zach stopped, out of breath, and rested his head on his arm. "You're just a fucking bike," he said.

His mom knew this house, knew it was where her husband had gone to get the syringe full of world-stopping drugs. She knew someone had lit her husband on fire on this street. And here Zach was, about to be arrested in front of the same house when all he had wanted were a few pills. Pills that doctors gave out, for fuck's sake. And he saw his mom's face again, her skin wrinkled in pain, heard her scream those same cries that kept him awake all night after their house was one person emptier.

The bike frame was just a red blur now, and a high-pitched hum came off the metal. Zach looked at the cop car, at the cold face of the man staring at him, and said, "All right, you piece of shit. You want to kill me? Kill me, but not here. Not in front of this house, please."

The cop car crept even closer. Close enough to see the oddly shaped head of the bald cop behind the wheel. And when Zach squinted, the cop looked like something other than a man, and those dark glasses hid something that gave him away for what he really was. Zach didn't know how he knew it, but he did.

The car came to a stop two houses down, and the bald cop's mouth was a thin line as he opened the door and stepped into the street. "Get off the bike and put your hands up!" he shouted.

Zach glanced down, tugged his hands. "I can't," he shouted back.

He swallowed hard as the cop's hand went to his waist. Zach heard a car door close behind him, and turned to see the other cop getting out of his vehicle. This one was tall with brown hair, and his head was tilted a little, looking past Zach to the bald cop.

"I said, get off the fucking bike, now!" the bald cop yelled again. His voice cracked a little and he crouched down, one leg in front of the other like he was going to start running at any second. And that one hand stayed at his waist, fingers curled.

Zach leaned down and whispered. "Not here. Take me back to the start. Come on," he wheezed, pushing down against the pedals, "let's ride some more you fucking piece of shit! Let's tear through time, go back to where it all went wrong."

As soon as the words left his mouth the red frame began to glow. So faint at first Zach thought he was imagining it. Then the front wheel started spinning, but the bike stayed right where it was. Smoke poured off the tire, filling Zach's nostrils with the smell of burnt rubber.

The bald cop took a few steps, staring at the spinning wheel. Zach couldn't see his eyes, but he guessed they'd be open as wide as they could go.

The vibrations grew so strong, and so loud, that Zach thought the bike might break down into molecules and atoms, just fly apart. All that metal and chrome singing a song. Something sparked beneath the front tire and flames spit out on the ground. Soon the whole wheel was on fire, burning a black mark on the asphalt. The tires spun faster and faster but the bike still didn't move.

The bald cop crouched in front of his car and a gun appeared in his hand so fast it looked like a magic trick. For a quick moment, Zach could see the cop's thoughts, could feel them floating in the air like dust through a beam of light. He *wanted* to pull his gun. He *wanted* to shoot it. All he needed was a reason, and Zach was giving it to him.

"Down on the ground, fucker!" the cop screamed.

Footsteps pounded behind Zach. He turned to see

the tall cop running forward, waving both hands in the air. This cop was yelling something, telling the bald cop to stand down. Telling him not to shoot. But his voice was lost in the squeal of the tires. Zach screamed too, because he didn't know what else to do and he didn't know what would happen next.

The vibrations rose in frequency until Zach's hands were a blur on the grips.

"Let's go, let's go!" Zach hissed.

The bike came unlocked and shot forward, a trail of fire on the ground behind it. Zach's upper body was pushed back so far his arms went completely straight. The place where his dad had burned and died was just a mirage on the street. Flames crawled up the frame, curled around the tank, and licked at Zach's arms.

He heard the bald cop yell again, but Zach couldn't understand it. Wind blew in his ears. The fire crackled as it caught the sleeve of Zach's sweatshirt. The tank between his knees was engulfed in flames.

The bike picked up speed, all that metal humming like some kind of infernal machine. The crisp wind stung the gash on Zach's forehead, but it felt good, it felt like being alive, even as he sped right at the bald cop and the dark open mouth of the gun pointed straight at him.

17

A searing pain burned Zach's legs as the flames from the bike moved up his body. Pain, like being scalded with hot water. Pain that burrowed down through his muscles and into his bones. He couldn't even see his jeans anymore, just the wind-whipped flames that boiled the skin of his calves, his thighs.

He screamed as loud as he could. Screamed so hard he tasted blood in his throat.

If the bald cop didn't move, Zach would crash right into him, and then the car behind him.

The thin line of the cop's mouth creased open to

show clenched teeth, and the barrel of the gun spit fire, then a loud crack echoed, bounced off the houses and cars.

Zach heard the sound immediately after something punched into his sternum. He coughed once. The bullet tore through Zach's chest and came bursting out his back in a gush of blood. The red liquid splashed onto the red paint of the bike, and Zach had just enough awareness to see his blood soak into the metal frame of a bike completely engulfed into flames. He sucked in a breath and felt air leaking out of the hole in his chest.

Then the bike came to a dead stop and released him.

Zach's hands and feet disconnected and he went weightless, flying through the air. One leg caught on the metal and carried the bike with him. His limp body smacked down onto the pavement and skidded, shredding skin from his face and hands. He came to a stop, his clothes on fire and his body twisted within the frame of the bike. One tire still spun uselessly. The street where he lay burned around him.

The fabric of his sweatshirt melted and dripped onto the skin of his back. Zach wanted to move, but he couldn't. He felt that his heart was emptied of blood, a dry pumping thing, slowing down. His throat filled with liquid and it ran down into his lungs with each breath. The world went monochromatic, then dimmed. He saw the sideways silhouette of the gray house, the sky behind it going dark. A shadow moved along the curtains of a second-story window, the same shape he saw when he'd taken the bike. The grit of asphalt ground into his cheek. His fingertips crawled along the pavement until he touched the smooth, melted patch of street where his dad had died.

Heavy footsteps pounded the road, but the sound grew more distant with each gasping breath.

I'm so sorry, Mom, he thought. *One more chance, that's all I needed. Just one more.*

Zach closed his eyes and his heart stopped.

18

A perfect circle of fire surrounded Zach's body, and the space inside it opened up. A gaping abyss in the asphalt that glowed with faint red light. The bike was pulled down into the hole, and Zach felt something inside him detach. A holographic version of himself slipped downward out of his body and fell into the abyss. His body lay up above— as though on a circle of clear glass—twisted, motionless, getting farther and farther away as he tumbled into oblivion. The curved walls of the tunnel pulsed with red veins.

A suffocating heat blew up into Zach's face, and it

burned, even though the part of him that felt pain was no longer alive. This was a deeper pain, something that shot right through his inner self and ignited everything that was left of him. He screamed as loud as he could, but the sound was lost in the rush of air as he fell.

Far below him, so far Zach thought he'd be falling for days, was a glowing red dot at the center of the all black. The heat grew stronger and Zach could not understand how he wasn't incinerated. He turned his head and looked back up the tunnel, but he couldn't even see the hole he'd fallen into.

The bike fell next to him, its bright red frame mangled from the crash. Zach reached out to touch it, to see if it was real, and his hand was transparent, as though he were nothing more than an outline. He looked down at the rest of his body and he recognized the shape of it, but it was being scattered by the velocity of the fall. Like a weak sand castle in a strong storm, the dust of his outline trailed behind him.

The heat was unbearable now, stifling. His tongue scratched the roof of his mouth, and when he swallowed his chest burned. The flickering red light at the bottom got bigger, clearer, and illuminated what appeared to be a giant cave of black earth.

The bottom came rushing up and Zach put his hands in front of his face to protect himself as his body slammed into the dirt floor. The shape of him burst apart into millions of pieces before slowly moving backward, as if drawn by a magnet, and reassembling. When his form had returned, Zach got to his knees just in time to see the bike smash into the ground next to him at full speed. On impact, the whole bike disintegrated into ash and it fell like snow, melted into the black dirt. Dirt that smelled of rot and decay.

He looked up, and there was nothing but pure darkness above him. In front of him was a large opening in the earth that curved out of view, and the wall at the far end glowed with red light.

Zach held out his hand again and looked more closely. He wasn't wrong in thinking this version of him was made of dust. His fingers were not fingers, but millions of shining silver grains of sand. They sparkled in the light, each one in motion. And somehow he knew, though he didn't know how, each grain represented moments and memories, lessons and connections. The very network of days, hours, minutes, and seconds that had made him who he was. It was all exposed, and it was all of him now. The body was gone and all that remained was...

My soul, Zach thought.

Not all of him was silver, though. Significant portions were darker than the rest. So black they were almost invisible, as though parts of him had been erased.

Except for his chest. Right in the center was a pulse of white that rippled outward, and when it did something like the sound of water rushed through his ears.

That was when Zach heard something echo from the cavern. A sound like the one Zach himself had made the night Dad died.

Crying.

A human voice weeping in anguish. Wailing, crying out. It sounded so much like his mom that Zach actually took a few steps toward the tunnel entrance and stopped.

He knew her cry. He had listened to it for weeks after Dad. A terrible howl followed by staccato groaning that made it sound like she was being punched in the gut. It cracked her voice and made her eyes so swollen he wondered if it would hurt to press the flesh around them.

Another voice joined to his mother's, and this one sounded just like Tessa, screaming into her pillow and weeping with so much force that Zach was afraid she might choke.

But it couldn't be them, could it? They were alive, still up there, under the sky. It was a lie, he knew it was, but still the sound made the dust of his being shiver and swirl like a flock of birds.

More voices joined in. Men, women. The raw wailing of an infant. A chorus. They grew in volume until it sounded like thousands of different people, all crying. Zach put his hands over his ears but it did nothing to drown out the noise.

There was motion in the tunnel, a shift in the light.

Zach backed away slowly as a shadow grew on the tunnel wall. A shape, a figure. The shadow crept up from the passage that angled down further into the earth. All Zach could see at first was the head. An oddly shaped head just like the cop's, like the shadow on the curtains of the gray house. Smooth and round, the temples curved inward, giving the head a skeletal look. The thin neck was attached to shoulders and arms so long Zach couldn't see the hands.

But as the shadow came closer, long sharp claws reached up to scratch along the ceiling of the tunnel. The upper body was also thin, but it was the legs that made Zach take a sharp inhale of the hot air. The legs were bent backward, its feet divided into two points, and it moved with staggered steps like a drawing on the pages of a flipbook.

A sound like hooves echoed off the walls as the shadow of the creature approached.

19

Everything that Zach was made of went cold, and he felt it more intensely than he had while he was alive. With the body stripped away, it was as though nerves were all that was left. Spiritual nerves that sent signals coursing throughout his rippling form.

The shadow jerked as the light of whatever fires lay down in the tunnel flickered. Zach backed away into the dark until his silver fingers pressed into the rank black dirt of the walls. Somewhere, far above him, was the street where his broken, bloodied body lay lifeless.

Had someone called to tell his mom yet? How

much time had passed?

He couldn't take his eyes off the shadow. It towered, black on the red wall, facing him but saying nothing. That strange white pulse kept rippling across Zach's chest, and each time there was rush of noise, like the ocean waves on Mom's sound machine. All of the other silver grains of sand trembled up and down Zach's legs as he stared at the figure.

Its head tilted and Zach had that same feeling as when the bald cop had looked at him. That every thought and fear was exposed, open to this creature.

A voice spoke, deep and smooth, and so low it was almost a whisper.

This is where you belong.

It wasn't a voice Zach heard, though. It was something he felt, coming from inside him. It resonated through those silver grains and he understood each and every word.

The path you chose, the choices you made, the voice said, *all lead here.*

The bent legs took a few steps forward. Firelight broke the shadow in half and it reformed, even larger now.

Zach didn't know if there was anything he could

do to stop whatever happened next, if all his chances had been used up, but he couldn't say nothing in return. He stepped away from the wall and tried to make his voice strong. The white pulse in his chest went faster.

"I just needed more time," he said, and even though no sound came out of his mouth, he heard his own voice the same way he heard the creature's.

And all would have ended the same, the shadow said.

The long, sharp claws curled on the wall, as if holding something and squeezing it.

"I would have made different choices," Zach said, "I would have done better."

One claw pointed at Zach.

You failed with the time you were given. Your mother and your sister were wounded, and did you comfort them, protect them? No. All you did was wound them further. Your own pain was all you ever saw, and it became so big that it made the world.

Zach slapped his glowing hands over his ears, where his ears should be, but the voice inside was just as loud as ever.

You are selfish, a failure, and now you have reached the end of the path you traveled.

The silver grains around Zach's knees crumbled

and he slipped to the ground. Muted gray dust fell from his eyes. He tried to picture his mom, Tessa, and he saw their faces briefly but they were fading.

"Is he…" Zach started, but the dust fell from his eyes faster and he found it hard to speak. "Is he here?"

The creature remained silent, and the claw turned from Zach and pointed down into the tunnel that was filled with fire and wailing. One voice rose above the others, a voice he'd longed to hear since it had been taken from him. His dad, weeping so brokenly that it twisted deep into Zach's neck with a sharp pain.

Zach put his hands over his face. Gray dust ran between his silver fingers and fell to the ground. Memories faded faster than he could hold on to them, but one of the last was seeing his father's burned body lying on Archer Way, his open eyes staring at nothing. And ever since then Zach had spent so many nights wondering where he was.

Mom said he was in heaven. But that wasn't true.

Maybe this *was* what he deserved. Maybe it was what they both deserved.

Zach slowly rose and faced the shadow. There was nothing he could say in his defense. Everything the creature said was true. He had been selfish. His own pain was so big that it completely covered him, wrapped him up in a dark blanket.

The white rippling in his chest stopped. So did the ocean noise. Now all he could hear were the screams, and the flames, and his own ragged breathing.

The shadow's claw curled in again, motioning for Zach to come closer. Zach took one step, and as his silver foot moved the whole tunnel lit up in a flash of bright light. There was a crack, like thunder, and blue veins of lightning coursed up the walls.

Something slammed into Zach's chest and his form was thrown backward. He stumbled to his feet and more light slashed the walls, so bright it left an afterimage. This time something pulled at his back, lifted him off the ground.

He floated in the air for a moment before crashing back down. His face hit the dirt and the smell of rotting meat and blood rushed up his nose. Zach looked up and saw the shadow on the wall, unmoving.

Thunder cracked again and this time there was an explosion of pain. Silver grains on his chest lit up with the same blue lightning as the walls. Something yanked him up into the air, then another burst of electricity and Zach shot up the tunnel as if pulled by an invisible wire.

The creature's voice came inside his head again, but it was fainter now.

You are what you are, and that will never change.

The fire glow from the cavern grew smaller, and the heat less scorching, as Zach flew upward. He twisted his head and saw a dark ceiling of dirt rushing toward him. He put his arms out, knowing that he would probably just shatter into a million grains of silver sand, but he slipped right through the earth.

20

Zach's eyes fluttered open and all he saw was gray.

A voice spoke, not in his head, but out loud.

"Son, can you hear me?"

Zach tried to lift his head but it wouldn't move. In fact, his whole body felt heavier, as though his skeleton was made of concrete instead of bone.

"Dad?" he said, and the word barely formed around a swollen tongue that tasted of blood and grit. "Dad, follow me back."

A blurry face leaned over him. The mouth moved. "Squeeze my hand if you can hear me."

Zach felt rough, gnarled skin wrap around his fingers and looked to see a strong, weathered hand gripping his own.

He looked back to the face, clearer now, and saw watery blue eyes, hair as white as a cloud. Zach gave a weak squeeze. Tears ran down the man's cheeks as he smiled. He put a hand over his heart, and the fingers were stained red with blood.

"It's not your time yet," the old man said. He squeezed Zach's hand again. "Keep on fighting."

The old man patted Zach's hand, then let go and his face went away. Another person appeared in his place, a young woman this time. Her face was tight, grim, and a stethoscope hung around her neck.

"That man…" Zach started.

"He lives across the street," the woman said. "He gave you chest compressions until we got here."

Zach's hand searched blindly for hers, but he couldn't find it.

"Is…" he began, but he wasn't sure how to ask the question. "Is all of me still there?"

The young woman avoided his eyes, and she wouldn't look at his body. Zach felt her cold, gloved hands wrap around his arm, pat the crook of his elbow.

"I'm starting an IV," she said. "Then I'll give you some medicine to help with the pain."

But Zach didn't have any pain, not yet. That would come later. For now, it felt like his soul, if that was what the scattered silver outline of himself had really been, had not quite reattached itself to his body. He tried to lift his head and it felt so heavy. He caught a glimpse of a burned sweatshirt, raw flesh, and two large pads attached to his chest, before his head lowered back down.

There was a stabbing pain in his arm, and moments later ice flooded his veins. The sky melted into swirls and Zach's heart beat wildly, erratically. This feeling, meds taking over his brain and wrapping the world in gauze— this, he promised himself, would be the last time he'd feel it. Whatever came next, whatever happened, he would experience all of it, no matter how much it hurt.

The young woman finally looked into Zach's eyes.

"Hang in there," she said. "Just a little longer."

Zach let his head fall back to the street, and he stared up at the sky as he was lifted onto a gurney. He was wheeled past two cops sitting on the sidewalk. One, he recognized, the tall cop who had pulled up behind him.

The other sat with his head hung, both hands covered his face and his shoulders shook. He glanced up as Zach went by and he looked nothing like the bald cop who had fired the gun. This man had blonde hair, no sunglasses. The cop's eyes met Zach's and his face fell apart. He cried harder as the tall cop put an arm around him.

The gurney was lifted into the ambulance and Zach saw the old man, standing between two black circles on the street. Zach tried to sit up, to look around the paramedics, but he couldn't see it. No red frame, no whitewall tires.

The bike was gone.

The old man, his blood covered hands folded together, watched as the paramedics went to work. He smiled the whole time, and even as the doors closed Zach could see him through the windows.

The old man shook his folded hands once, twice, as though cheering Zach on. Then the sirens kicked in and wailed and Zach slipped into unconsciousness, but his soul kept dreaming.

21

Four Months Later

Zach Ayers woke up before the sun. He showered and shaved, then paused while slipping on a black polo shirt with the words "Fagan's Grocery" embroidered over the left breast. He turned his back to the mirror and looked over his shoulder so he could see the knotted flesh of his back, the twisted scars where he had been burned. His entire back, from the waistband of his boxers up to his neck, a map to some unnamed place.

The skin grafts, taken from his thigh, had helped

cover up some of the worst burns, but there was no hiding what had happened. At first, he had hated the sight of the scars. They were ugly, a deformity, but he'd spent so much time looking at them that now he couldn't picture himself without them.

Facing the mirror now, he touched the folded skin where the bullet had entered, traced the small holes where the staples had held it back together. He leaned in closer to the mirror and touched his crooked nose.

After tucking in his shirt and cinching his belt, Zach went to his room and took a nametag off the dresser. He slipped the pin into the fabric of his shirt and clasped it.

He pulled the comforter up on his bed and smoothed it out. Then he got on his knees, stuck his arm underneath the bed, and searched until his fingers touched the cold metal of his Superman lunch box.

The lid creaked open and Zach stared at the large stack of cash he'd manage to save. He'd never had so much money in his entire life. He wasn't sure what he'd do with it, but he'd figure something out in time. Maybe a vacation for the three of them. Somewhere sunny and warm.

Tessa still wasn't awake yet, so he closed his bedroom door softly and went down the hall to the kitchen.

He'd have to get her up soon if she didn't get up on her own.

After pouring himself a cup of coffee, Zach took out some bread, turkey, cheese, and pickles, and made two sandwiches. One went into Tessa's lunchbox, the other into his own. He added a package of crackers and some string cheese to hers, and then as he was zipping it up, pulled open the snack drawer, took out a small piece of chocolate, and tossed it in the lunchbox.

Zach looked at the clock on the stove. He had just enough time to get Tessa on the bus and head over to the coffee shop to meet up with Henry Thayer, the man who had given him chest compressions. The man who had saved his life. And, as Zach found out in the hospital when Mr. Thayer came to visit him, he was there when the ambulance came for his dad. He had been one of the figures sitting on the curb that Zach barely noticed.

Now, they had coffee at least once a week. Zach would tell him about problems with coworkers, the girl he liked who came into the store, and Thayer would listen, offer advice.

Zach went to Tessa's room and woke her up, guided her still halfway-sleeping body to the bathroom, and told her to take a shower. As he walked down the hall he heard the front door open and close, and the sound of keys being dropped onto the counter.

He went out into the kitchen to find his mom standing at the open refrigerator, taking a swig of orange juice straight from the carton.

She put down the juice and wiped her mouth with her sleeve. She smelled of cleaning chemicals and powdered gloves. Her black curly hair had gone white at the temples, but Zach thought she looked more beautiful than she had since Dad died.

"Morning," he said, wrapping his arms around her. She hugged him back, hard, as she had every day since he'd been discharged from the hospital.

She pulled back and ran a hand along his shirt. "You need to iron this," she said.

Zach smiled and kissed her cheek. "Sleep well," he said.

His mother's eyes fluttered with fatigue. She kissed her fingertips, then pressed them to Zach's lips. While Zach poured coffee into a thermos he heard the door to her bedroom close, and the ocean noise of her sound machine filled the hall.

Thayer was already at the coffee shop when Zach arrived. The older man stood with a quick groan and gave Zach a hug. They sat at a table by the window, watched as a garbage truck drove by a small homeless city made of tents, tarps, and shopping carts.

Thayer told Zach the cops had finally raided the gray house on Archer Way a few days ago—a house, Thayer said, he had called about many times before—but when the police arrived the place was empty. Hundreds of people had stopped by that house, gone inside and come back out barely able to walk, eyes glazed over. But the cops told Thayer it looked like the house hadn't been lived in for years. They couldn't find any evidence of a tenant, let alone drugs.

Last night, Thayer told him, he had sat in his favorite chair by the window and watched as a car pulled up to the gray house. None of the lights were even on. Someone got out, went up to the door, knocked, and the door opened but there was no one inside. Nothing but a faint red glow.

Five or ten minutes went by and this person came

back out, got in the car, and drove way.

"Whatever people want," Thayer said, "they'll find a way to get it."

Zach asked if he was going to call the cops again.

"Oh, I've thought about it," Thayer said. "But I have a feeling the place would be just as empty as it was when they searched it."

Zach was going to ask what he meant, but Thayer's eyes grew wet and he stared out the window, chewing on his lip.

"What are you thinking, old man?" Zach asked.

"Alice," Thayer said, "and time. Mostly Alice, though."

He sighed and lifted a hand to his face to wipe moisture from his eyes.

"When you love someone," Thayer said, "however much time you have with them is never enough. Young, old, doesn't matter. You always want more."

Zach nodded like he understood. And maybe he did, a little.

"I see her sometimes," Thayer said, spinning his coffee cup in slow circles. "She floats through the house reliving a day that's long gone. And I sit there in my chair and watch her, ask myself why it's this one day she's acting out."

He lifted the cup, stared into the black liquid for a second, and took a drink.

"Maybe that's what she's trying to tell me. It's just a nothing day, but it's not nothing. It's a day when she was alive and we were together. She always told me something bad would happen because of that house. It's too bad she never got to see the good that came because of it, too."

Thayer smiled, reached across the table, and put a blue-veined, liver-spotted hand on top of Zach's scarred hand. "Somehow, you got more of that one thing we all want but can never get."

After they finished their coffee, Zach stood up, putting most of his weight on the left leg, took both cups, and limped over to the counter, where he set them down.

"You're still walking like an old man," Thayer said with a smile when Zach came back.

Zach put a hand to his leg, pushed down where the pain was, but his fingers could never reach it. Physical therapy was helping, but sometimes he swore he could feel the pins and screws that held his shattered bone together.

"Still got all my hair though," Zach said, as he

and Thayer walked outside into the cold. Thayer laughed, rubbed his head, and said, "Just you wait. Time will catch up eventually."

Zach shivered and zipped up his coat, glanced at his watch. "I've got to get going," he said. "But I'll stop by this weekend, if that's okay."

Thayer reached out and put a hand on Zach's shoulder. "Listen, I know it's a hard thing to take, not being to play basketball anymore. But I've found that sometimes life has another thing waiting for us just behind the thing we've lost. Give it some time, tell me if I'm wrong."

Thayer's blue eyes were clear and shining with tears as he pulled Zach in and embraced him. "Make this a day worth living, young man. And tomorrow, do it again."

He pulled away, gave Zach a smile, turned, and walked down the street. Zach watched him for a few seconds, then pulled the straps tighter on his backpack, and began the walk to work.

Zach walked in the morning light of an orange sky, taking deep breaths of the crisp air. Four months since the "accident," (what else could he call it?) and two months since his last pill. He had to take some after the surgeries to deal with the pain, and to his surprise, Zach didn't have any desire for the meds. Sometimes he missed the soft explosion in his head when they kicked in, but for the most part he didn't really think about it.

After he got out of the hospital and had recovered enough to get a job, his mom had offered to buy him a bike so he could ride to work, but he told her he preferred walking, which at the time had been a lie, but was now true. He liked having his feet on the ground.

As Zach neared an intersection he heard muffled shouting in the distance, coming closer. He stopped and listened. The voice sounded familiar, even though he couldn't quite think of why. The shouting sounded again, louder this time.

Then he saw it, tearing down the center of the street, a red bike with a frame that looked like an old Schwinn, but different. The man riding it wore a gray three-piece suit that was torn and frayed. His white face mask was askew and stained red around the mouth.

The man turned toward Zach as the bike went by. One eye was nearly swollen shut, dark blood leaked from his hair in red lines. His one good eye looked at Zach, open as wide as it would go. The man shouted again, but the bike was going so fast that the words were lost.

The bike tore past Zach and a hot wind followed close behind.

"Hazard?" Zach yelled after him. "Hazard!"

Zach dropped his coffee mug and started running, shouting after Hazard. He didn't know if he could catch up to the bike, but he had to try. If only because he wished there had been someone to chase after him.

But the bike had already turned down another street, carrying its new passenger and racing him away into whatever hell waited for him.

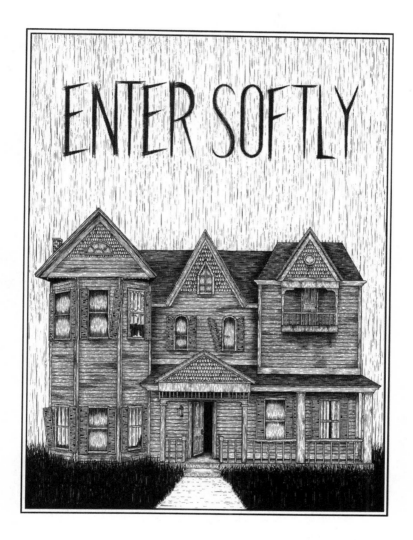

1

Lisa Morton stood just outside the Emergency Department of Emmanuel hospital in downtown Portland, cellphone pressed so tight against her ear she was getting a headache.

"How can he do that?" she said. Her hand clenched into a fist and unclenched. Over and over.

The woman's voice on the other end, patient, gentle, explained exactly how *he* could do that.

"It was one time," Lisa almost yelled. "One mistake!"

She watched as an ambulance pulled up to the round. Two paramedics jumped out, lowered a stretcher to the ground, and wheeled it through the glass double doors that opened with a pneumatic wheeze.

"One mistake is all it takes," her lawyer said. "Listen, I know you have to go to work, and I'm sorry to give you this news right before you start your shift."

Lisa breathed fast, could feel the skin on her neck start to itch as angry blood rushed through her.

"He's my son," she said. "He means more to me than he ever meant to Mark. Has anyone asked Sean who he wants to be with?"

The lawyer started speaking, but Lisa interrupted.

"Have they? Sit Sean down in a room without his fucking dad right there, and ask him. You know what he'll say."

A pregnant girl, young, about to burst by the look of her protruding stomach, waddled to the ED with a much older man next to her. The man seemed agitated, not at all concerned or compassionate. Lisa hoped he wasn't the father, but experience told her he probably was.

In just a few hours that bump would be gone, and new life would come screaming into the world. Blood-covered and vulnerable, seeing only vague shapes instead of faces, unable to recognize words, only voices.

The thought cracked Lisa's anger, and sadness

came seeping through like water in a leaking boat.

"How is he?" she asked, her voice shaking. "Sean, I mean. How is he doing?"

The lawyer sighed. Not a sigh of annoyance, but because she had to answer a question that would only cause more pain.

"He's still got the cast," the lawyer said. "Got it signed by all his friends at school. You can't even tell he had black eyes. They're all healed up."

The lawyer paused, took a sip of water. Lisa could hear her swallow and swallowed herself unconsciously.

"I need to tell you something," the lawyer said. "You're going to find out eventually, but I want you to hear it from me."

She paused again, and Lisa moved out of the way as two men dressed in filthy clothes stumbled past her. One holding onto the other. Their smoke-scratched voices mumbling nothing she could understand. A stench of body odor and weed followed as they went by.

The lawyer spoke. "Sean said there's a woman who has been staying at the house, helping take care of him."

"A nurse?" Lisa asked.

"A friend of Mark's is how Sean put it. Everything

he told me makes it sound like she's a girlfriend, Lisa."

The red glowing letters that spelled out EMERGENCY DEPARTMENT bled together into a bright, red mess. Lisa wasn't even aware of the tears that ran down her face. Her pulse pounded at the back of her skull.

"I knew it, I fucking knew it," she said. "That asshole has been sneaking around for months, just waiting for me to mess up so he could take Sean and be done with me."

The muscles in the arm that held the phone started to tighten and cramp. Lisa let the phone down from her ear for a moment, and the lawyer's voice, trying to soothe her, went down with it. She looked up into the black sky, layered with thin white clouds. Her breath rose like smoke, and she wondered if that was her soul, finally leaving her too. Slipping away, bit by bit, until there was nothing left of the Lisa Morton she used to be.

Lisa put the phone back to her ear and tried to calm her breathing.

"Have you seen her?" Lisa asked. "What does she look like? Is she pretty? Is she——"

"Lisa," the lawyer said. "Stop."

That's when the real tears came, and these Lisa felt. They came from deep inside, down in her guts, and pushed out through her eyes painfully, as though it was too much liquid for her tear ducts to handle. Before she knew what was happening, she was doubled over, clutching her stomach and sobbing until it felt like she'd done a hundred sit-ups. Her pulse pounded louder, this time in her temples, behind her eyes. She wailed, right there in front of the Emergency Department as a teenage boy, wrist bent all sideways, walked by with his mom. Neither of them looked at Lisa or asked if she was okay. And this made her cry even harder.

"There's one more thing," the lawyer said. "And I need you to listen very carefully."

Lisa straightened up, wiped her eyes. "Okay."

"The judge asked Sean how he fell down the stairs."

Sound disappeared from the world, and the sky itself seemed to curve around her like the glass of a snow globe. Maybe, if someone shook the earth, massive snowflakes would rise from the ground to float in the air.

"What...what did he say?" Lisa asked.

The lawyer sighed. "Sean said you were drunk, and he was trying to get away from you. You yelled and chased him up the stairs. You grabbed his sweatshirt when he was near the top and pulled him back. He lost his balance and went all the way down."

"But that's not true!" Lisa shouted.

"Lisa," the lawyer said. "That's how Sean sees it, and you need to understand that. He can't see your reasons or your heart. All he knows is that his mother was acting strange and tried to hurt him."

Anger welled up inside Lisa again, but this time it was directed only at herself. She'd spent a good chunk of her life wondering if she had any worth, any value. All those dark days in high school and college seemed to end when she met Mark, built a life with him, and started her career.

When had she started feeling worthless again? Was it before or after she suspected Mark was cheating?

"Before," Lisa said out loud.

"Excuse me?" the lawyer said.

Lisa had come to believe that there was a black hole inside her brain, and every good thought, every positive intention, got sucked right into it. Never to be seen again. And this left her lost, hopeless. She'd been feeling that way the night she hurt Sean. She'd taken some pills and drank some wine. She just wanted to sleep, and she wanted her son to love her. She never meant to do what she did.

"That's how he sees it," Lisa said.

"Yes," the lawyer said gently. "He needs time to heal, and so do you, I think. If what he says is even partially true, Lisa, you need to get things back on track. Rehab if necessary. If you want to see your son again, you need to do what's best for him. Which, in this case, is also what's best for you."

Maybe someone did shake the earth and float up all the snow because a chill ran down Lisa's back. Her heart stopped pounding in her skull, and the headache went away. She had always heard that drowning was a peaceful way to die. The mind eventually accepts the water into the lungs—like the body remembers being an infant submerged in amniotic fluid—and slips away without fighting. That's what Lisa felt, now. Like drowning, without any water in sight.

"I understand," Lisa said and hung up the phone.

She knew what she was, what she'd always be.

Lisa slipped the phone into her purse, clipped her badge to her scrub top, and walked into Emmanuel hospital to start her shift as an Emergency Department nurse.

2

Lisa was stationed in the Green Pod with Patrick and Meagan. She didn't mind Meagan so much. She was nice enough, but God, her life was so perfect. Husband did something with stocks, their two small children were beautiful enough to be models, and every picture she posted online looked like it was taken by a professional. Beautiful house, weekends at the beach, perfectly prepared meals.

And Patrick, he was just an asshole. Lazy too. But Lisa didn't mind that tonight. She needed to keep busy, keep moving. Let Patrick sit, legs all spread, staring at his phone with dead eyes. Hard to believe he was married. Probably the kind of guy who just laid on the couch and watched football all weekend. His wife would cheat on him eventually if she weren't already.

The first patient of the night was an elderly man with chest pain. He came by ambulance and was rushed into the room where a tech hooked up EKG wires, and a phlebotomist drew blood. Both the EKG and blood work confirmed a heart attack, so the patient was taken to the Cath Lab, where he'd have a catheter pushed into his artery to search for blockages. He'd be admitted to the hospital afterward, which meant he was no longer Lisa's problem.

The second patient was a three-year-old with a cough. Lisa wanted to scream at the mom that a cold did not qualify as an "emergency," but she bit her tongue.

There was pressure in Lisa's head, in the space right next to that black hole of depression, and she knew exactly what it meant. It was just a finger poking her brain right now, but soon it would turn into a thought and then a need. A pill, a drink. Something to shrink that black hole, make it less hungry.

Lisa turned her thoughts to Sean, to her son in his cast. She shook her head until her eyes went blurry, then got back to work.

The night wore on into the early morning.

A teen girl with a sprained ankle.

A man who attempted a half-hearted suicide by swallowing fifty aspirin.

A woman who sliced her finger to the bone while chopping carrots.

An old woman who passed out when she got up to pee.

On and on.

When Lisa was caring for the old woman, she noticed a bottle of pills in the purse on the chair next to the bed. She could just see the letters V-I-C-O and knew immediately what the other letters would be. Lisa had read in the woman's chart that she'd broken a toe two months earlier, and that bottle of pills was most likely the Vicodin her doctor had prescribed for pain.

Orange bottle, white cap. A beautiful little pop when you worked the cap off with your thumb. White pills, bitter on the tongue. A subtle dizziness once they were swallowed and dissolved. Lisa could imagine the feeling exactly. Her hand moved, actually twitched, at the thought of reaching into the purse and taking the bottle. A woman that old, she'd blame herself for their disappearance. Was probably misplacing things all the time.

Lisa took the woman's blood pressure, wrote the number down on a piece of paper, and left the room, still feeling a little dizzy.

She went to her computer and finished the charting for her last discharged patient. The ED was quiet, still. Meagan was in a room with a patient, and Patrick's thumb was working overtime, scrolling endlessly through pictures of someone else's life. There was something in the air, though. Faint. A feeling at first, but then a smell.

Fire? Burning? Cooking?

Lisa stood, tilted her nose up, and sniffed. Something burned, definitely. Something else in the air, like static electricity, went over the back of her neck and made the hairs rise. She shivered and looked down at her arms. They were covered in goosebumps.

Then the screaming started.

The door from the ambulance entrance burst open, and two male paramedics came into the department pushing a stretcher. Each of them had one hand on the stretcher and the other trying to hold down a thrashing patient.

The patient, mid-twenties Lisa guessed from the patchy facial hair and band t-shirt he wore, screamed with all his strength. His head was thrust back against the cushion, and Lisa could see all the cords in his neck as his voice echoed down the hallway.

It wasn't until the paramedics wheeled him closer that Lisa saw why he was screaming. His legs, if they could even be called that anymore, were covered in hard, black skin. Skin that was split open in long cracks that revealed bright, red flesh underneath. He had no shoes on, and the jeans he wore had been cut off just above the knees, probably by the paramedics, but there were still bits of fabric fused with the hardened skin.

When the smell hit her nose, Lisa had to turn her head and gag. It wasn't so much that the smell was bad—although it was, but she had smelled worse—it was that the overcooked, meat-like odor that made her think of food, was, in fact, human flesh. Roasted and charred like something that had been left on the grill too long.

The man continued screaming as the paramedics rushed him into a room, then used the blanket he lay on like a hammock to lift him to the hospital bed. Flakes of black skin and dark blood stains dotted the blanket. As the man thrashed, more pieces of hardened skin were torn off, leaving wounds leaking fresh blood. Tubing ran from the patient's arm to an IV bag that a paramedic hung on a pole.

Doctor Ferris came into the room, followed by Patrick and Meagan, each carrying supplies. Ferris took a stethoscope from around his neck and told the still screaming patient he needed to listen to his lungs. He leaned over the burned man, but Lisa guessed all the doctor heard was the patient's voice, echoing inside his chest.

Ferris straightened, looked at Lisa. "Let's get some fentanyl on board and some ice packs to cool the legs."

Lisa nodded and left the room, grateful to get away from the screaming and the stench. Thirteen years as a nurse, and there were still some things she couldn't stomach. She went over to the medication unit—a sort of metal dresser with locked drawers, a computer screen, and a refrigerated section with a glass door—and punched in her code. She selected fentanyl from the list, entered the dosage, and one of the drawers hissed open. Lisa grabbed the syringe and slid the drawer shut.

She ran over to the supply room, grabbed as many cold packs as she could carry, and returned to the patient's room. The screaming had stopped now, and more people were gathered around the bed—aides, respiratory therapists, residents. Lisa shouldered her way through the small crowd and reached the patient. The man's eyes were open wide, wider than Lisa had ever seen someone open their eyes before. There was way too much white. He stared straight up at the ceiling, the muscles in his throat quivering, mouth opening and closing. The skin on his face had turned an icy blue. She heard a wheeze, like a winter wind coming through a cracked window.

Ferris stood looking at the EKG monitor with a frown.

"He's going into V-fib," he said. "We need to intubate and get the pads on him."

Lisa put the syringe of fentanyl into her pocket as someone wheeled in the crash cart. She ripped open the package of defibrillator pads, waited until the aide cut open the patient's shirt with a pair of sheers, then slapped the pads on his chest. A respiratory therapist leaned over the patient and shoved a curved metal blade into his mouth. The therapist guided a tube down his throat, then connected an Ambu bag and began squeezing it.

"Okay," Ferris said, "everyone, back away."

Lisa and the therapist did as they were told, and the patient lay exposed on the bed, eyes still wide but unblinking now. The heart monitor beeped too fast. A robotic voice from the defibrillator said, *"Analyzing rhythm."*

Looking at the patient's legs, Lisa wasn't sure if the man would ever walk again, even if he made it through the night. The burns were much deeper than she had realized when she first saw him. The split flesh along his calves and thighs reminded her of the volcano she and Mark had visited on their honeymoon in Hawaii. Black volcanic rock cracked open to reveal the hellish glow of lava flows beneath, twisting and curving like streams of the earth's blood.

The robotic voice spoke again.

"Shock advised."

"Clear," Ferris said.

"Clear," Lisa repeated. Her voice was quiet and distant.

Ferris pushed the lightning bolt button on the machine, and the robot said, *"Stand back. Delivering shock."*

Lisa knew what was coming, had seen it a thousand times or more, but it still made her feel something she couldn't quite name. Sadness, maybe. The patient's body jerked upward off the bed, then fell limp back onto the sheets. The beeping heartbeat stopped, became a droning noise. Lisa looked at the monitor and saw only a thin, green line marching across the screen.

"Start compressions," Ferris said.

Lisa leaned over the patient, lifeless now, the eyes a little less wide but still open. The light was gone from them, and she'd seen that a thousand times as well. It rarely came back once it left. The spirit, the soul, whatever you wanted to call it. Once the body failed, it took flight, went wherever it went, and the group of people inside this cold room went to work on a shell of flesh and blood, trying desperately to make the stilled machinery do something it no longer wanted to do.

She put one hand over the other on the patient's chest, still warm. She laced her fingers together and pressed down as hard as she could. She felt the crack of the man's ribs, and the bones loosened up, became more pliable so she could squeeze the heart between the sternum and spine to artificially pump oxygen-filled blood through his body.

In CPR classes, they'd always been taught to give compressions at one hundred beats per minute, and it helped if you did it to the rhythm of a song. But Lisa never could hear a song in her head as she pushed down again and again on a dying patient's chest, so she told herself that maybe the next pump, or the next, or the next, would be the one to revive the person.

She did thirty compressions, stepped back, and let the respiratory therapist squeeze the Ambu bag twice. The patient's chest rose and fell each time. Then Lisa went right back to the compressions, feeling the tough muscle of the heart give way with each push. She could almost sense the blood moving through endless tunnels.

She glanced at the patient's face, blinked hard. She wished his eyes were closed. She felt like the man was watching her with a melancholy expression.

Can you bring me back, Lisa? Keep on pumping. Don't give up just yet.

The voice she heard, though, was Mark's. A voice that used to soothe and calm her when she felt stressed.

Come on, Lisa. You can do it.

Tears stung her eyes as she thought of her husband, pictured him with another woman. Pictured their son in his cast. Did she still love Mark? Yes, maybe she did. After all, what would she have done if Mark was the one who got drunk and high and accidentally pulled their son down the stairs? She'd probably leave him, too.

She lost count of how many compressions she'd

done, but it didn't matter. She thought she saw the patient's lips start to turn upward in a slight smile as if to say, *You're doing so good. Don't stop now.*

Mark, who had stood by her side and loved her when she felt like nothing. Less than nothing. But she never could fight all those inner voices that told her she was a failure and not worth loving.

She pushed even harder now, faster. The muscles in her arms burned as she pressed the patient's heart down, let it fill back up with blood only to push it down again.

A gloved hand touched her arm, and she was aware of the sensation, but she didn't stop. Couldn't stop. Sweat ran down her face. She pushed more, and more, and more. The constant pressure made the patient's skin raw, and blood leaked out from under Lisa's hands. Made her gloves slick and sticky.

Someone said her name, but the patient's lips turned up even more, and was that light coming back into his eyes? Yes, it was! Somewhere beneath all that blood and bone was a heart, and maybe if she pumped it long enough, she could bring it back to life. The patient, her marriage, *her* life. All of it.

She pressed down, again and again. The

hand on her arm squeezed, but she barely felt it. She heard her name again, but she couldn't stop, not until she had put the blood back into all the things that had died.

3

After Doctor Ferris called the time of death, the body was covered with a sheet, and the heavy glass door slid shut. Not just for privacy but to keep the stench from floating down the hall. Even so, Lisa could still smell it, and it made her even sicker to know that the man to whom it belonged was no longer alive.

After the man died, Meagan put her arm around Lisa and told her to take a break, pull herself together. So Lisa did just that. She locked herself in the staff bathroom, put her back against the wall, and slid down to the floor. She expected to cry, to let out all the pent-up emotion, but nothing came. Just heaviness.

Spiritual. She didn't know how else to describe

it. It came from inside, a big, cold shadow that covered all her thoughts. She tried to think of Sean, her son, in a cast because of her. But even that didn't trigger tears. Everything she loved had this enormous weight connected to it—her son, her marriage, her job, even her soul—pulled down by these heavy weights that stretched and contorted everything good until it was nothing but a thinned-out, torn reason for existing.

Lisa reached into her pocket—for what, she didn't know—and felt the syringe of fentanyl she'd pulled out of the medication machine for the dead man. So many nurses she knew had slipped a pill here and there. Sometimes the doctor would order pain meds, and the patient would refuse, or maybe the doc ordered three pills, and only one did the trick. But what she held in her hand was enough to blast her consciousness off planet earth. Enough medication to numb the pain of a burn victim so injured it caused his death.

She held up the syringe, looked at the cloudy liquid in the harsh bathroom light. A solution or a problem? Self-medicating. It wasn't a problem until it was. And when did that happen? Was there a blurry line between everything-is-okay and everything-is-shit? A line you don't even know is there until you've crossed it?

She crossed that line with Sean. She knew that now. If she was honest, she had probably been dancing on the edge for months, if not longer, before the night she pulled her son down the stairs. Watched as his small body tumbled down each step. She vaguely remembered the wave of nausea and fear pop in her chest like a burst balloon when she heard the snap of his bone. She was trying not to cry, but he couldn't breathe, and his arm hung there all limp and grotesque.

She had tried to ice the break, hadn't she? Why? Because she didn't want to call 911. She sure as hell couldn't drive, and she knew there was no way she could fake sobriety under the experienced eyes of paramedics. So she prolonged her son's pain. She pulled a bag of frozen vegetables from the freezer and held it against Sean's swollen arm. Slurring apologies the whole time. By then, the bruises on his face had started to bloom like evil flowers.

So she made the call.

First, the ambulance showed up. Then cops.

Her lawyer was right. She had already lost everything important to her. But it wasn't gone completely. There was still a chance she could get it back. She had to try. She had to believe that she was not the sum of all the worst things she had ever done. She could change, be better. For Sean, maybe even for Mark. She loved him, still.

Lisa slipped the syringe back into her pocket and looked up. Her face in the mirror startled her. The skin under her eyes was swollen, outlined by wrinkles, and when had those strands of gray become so visible?

She looked haunted…or hunted.

Hunted by this black dog, she called depression. Chased since she was in junior high by this slobbering, hungry beast that bit at her ankles would drag her into unhappiness if it grabbed hold.

She remembered a moment from almost a year ago, before the incident with Sean, before Mark's love was hidden. She had been feeling down for days, and she couldn't figure out why. That black hole in her head sucked in all joy, all happiness until she felt like there was a rainstorm inside her. A torrential downpour that drowned and washed away everything good.

She had been lying in bed for days, staring at the wall, barely eating, when Mark came in to ask how she was feeling. She mumbled something, and Mark asked her to begin naming the good things in her life.

She hated the question. Hated that he wanted her to speak, to think.

She said, "Please, just leave me alone."

And Mark, the man she loved, gently ran his fingers through her hair and said, "Do you remember when the life we have now was the life you dreamed about? We got married, we found good jobs, we bought a house. And we have an amazing son. We built a life, a family."

Lisa tried not to let the tears come, but they did. Where were all of those things in her head? Why couldn't she feel them?

And now, standing in the staff bathroom, she smiled into the mirror, eyes half-closed.

She knew the sadness would never really go away, but she'd found a way to make it bearable, and maybe that's all anyone ever did. Maybe the happiest-looking people she saw online were all drunk, medicated, high. How else could they get through this life? Unless...unless...they didn't have holes in their heads.

The smiling face that looked back at her from the mirror changed, distorted. The eyes narrowed, and the lips curled up. The smile remained, but it now looked like the face of someone who had done something awful but didn't regret it one bit.

Lisa stepped back from the mirror, but the reflection stayed exactly where it was. Staring at her with unblinking eyes. The mouth turned even more, and now the smile was more like a snarl. The lips peeled back to reveal short sharp teeth.

Lisa closed her own eyes and backed away until she hit a wall. She counted to ten, then did it backward. When she opened her eyes, the face in the mirror was gone, but her heart still felt like it was lodged in her throat.

She put both hands on her knees and started to laugh. It was the only thing she could do because otherwise, she would start to cry.

She stepped back to the mirror, opened her mouth wide, made a funny face. The person in the mirror did the same thing. Satisfied that no one else was in the glass, Lisa turned on the faucet, cupped her hand under the cold water, and splashed it on her neck. It felt good.

When she left the bathroom, Lisa felt something she had not felt in a long time. Pride. She had stared straight at temptation and turned her back on it. She would not have done that last week, or yesterday for that matter. She tried to think of things she'd overheard some of the psychologists tell patients who were struggling with addiction.

Sobriety is not just one decision. It is a series of decisions made over days, weeks, months.

An addict is what you are. A person who is clean and sober is what you *choose* to be.

If that was true, she had to choose to be something better for her son. He deserved more than what she was.

4

Out in the hall, she passed a custodian wiping down an empty room. The smell of alcohol-based cleaners drifted out of the room, made her think of vodka. And speaking of smells, the odor of burned flesh was still really strong in the unit. Shouldn't it be fading by now?

She walked by Patrick at the nurse's station. A website with a bunch of tennis shoes glowed on the screen. He followed Lisa with his eyes and a slight smile.

Fucking creep.

Her steps quickened, and she avoided looking right at him.

Shit, that smell was even stronger now. She stuck her head in the room where the man had died. The man who had been burned to death. How or why, not even the paramedics knew.

A crew had come and deep-cleaned the room, spraying every surface, corner, and piece of equipment with an eye-burning disinfectant, and that was all Lisa could smell inside.

So, where was the smell coming from?

The man who had been burned up in a fire was now good and cold in a morgue refrigerator. Hot to cold. Why was that funny? It wasn't, and Lisa knew it. But she couldn't stop herself from laughing. Was it ironic? Was that word? Or just one of those strange facts of life that happen to have some symmetry to it?

Lisa backed out of the room. She stopped laughing when she saw Meagan staring at her. Perfect Meagan with her perfect everything. God damn her and her perfect husband. All the stories that Meagan told about him were probably lies. Probably the things she wished he would do. No husband was that loving, that attentive unless he'd been caught cheating or something. Which Lisa hoped was the case. She hoped Meagan's husband was out with someone at that very moment. Someone uglier than Meagan because that would really put a knife through that bitch's ego. Slit the throat of her thin, meaningless life of furniture, beach trips, wine nights with girlfriends, and endless social media photographs of her smiling like she was in a dental ad.

Good God, that smell.

The odor hit Lisa right in the gag reflex, and she burped a bitter taste. She realized she'd forgotten to eat dinner again. With no one to cook for, she didn't care about food these days. So, she'd pop a sleeping pill, wash it down with some vodka, and then stalk her husband on social media. Hoping, not hoping he'd post something she could sharpen and use against her sense of self-righteousness.

She was wrong, and she knew it. But if she accepted that, what did it mean for the fragile structure she'd built around herself?

A howl echoed down the hallway. It froze Lisa in mid-step and instantly made her skin go cold. As cold as a body in the morgue.

She looked over to Meagan, but she was busy typing notes in a patient's chart. She didn't move or even act like she heard it. Same with Patrick. He was still clicking away with a bored expression. Those heavy-hooded eyes always made him look condescending.

There it was again, but this time it was familiar.

Lisa knew that voice recognized it. She knew it because it was the same voice she heard when the burned man first came in. Wheeled in on that stretcher, screaming. It was such an awful, hideous expulsion of pure pain that she couldn't forget it.

An echo. That's what it is. Time bending into a fucking circle. The smell, the sound, it's all coming back around again.

The lights flickered above her head, and why wasn't Meagan moving anymore? She just sat there, fingers hanging above the keyboard, a blank expression. Frozen. Patrick too. The lights flickered some more, strobing from the ceiling and then again on the polished tile floor.

The double doors down the hallway slowly opened, and the howl came sneaking in through that open space, rushing in with another wave of nausea. The stench of burned flesh, meat cooked until the skin hardened into a black shell and cracked open to reveal the red underneath.

Lisa's heart sped up and moved adrenaline faster through her system. Her feet were stuck to the floor. She tried to move her legs but couldn't. She did not want to see that man again. She had told herself she was fine when he was wheeled into the room the first time, but she wasn't. He seemed to her a physical representation of all the pain, all the torched parts of herself that were so far beyond repair it was a wonder she was even still alive. There was a destroyed, burned person inside Lisa Morton, and watching that man writhe in agony, screaming for God, his mother, father, anyone and everyone—it was too much for her.

And here he came again. Feet first through those double doors. But they weren't really feet, were they? The fire must have started there because most of the flesh was burned off the feet and toes. They were just skeletal shapes covered in strips of tough, black skin. Misshapen and cruel. Those ragged things pushed uselessly against the bed as the patient twisted and turned, and there was no mistaking it now. It was the same man. The same one who was now in the morgue.

Lisa, stuck in place, could not figure out for the life of her how the man had managed to resurrect himself, escape the morgue, and then go out and get lit on fire again. Only the men pushing the stretcher were not paramedics. At least they were dressed like it. Were those robes? No, sheets. Bed sheets, like what she'd use on the hospital bed. Bleached white, with a few rusty brown stains that wouldn't come out. Starched stiff and scratchy, these figures (because she wasn't sure they were men anymore) were covered in sheets. One wrapped around each body, another around the shoulders, and a third pulled over the head like a hood. What she could see of the faces reminded her of clay. A skull smothered in clay and smoothed out. Gray skin and thin lips. Deep-set eyes that were black and lifeless. These figures moved with the stretcher. Lisa couldn't see their feet, but they seemed to glide along the floor.

The patient howled again, and his body jerked upright until he was looking straight at Lisa. His eyes were filled with blood, open so wide it looked like two red hot coals shoved into his sockets. His shriveled legs twitched, moving as though they didn't belong to him. Like they were the ruined pieces of some other patient, abandoned on this stretcher, still kicking with frayed nerve endings. This patient looked right at her with his red eyes and screamed so loud she thought her ears drums might rupture. She saw more than just pain in the man's face. She saw fear. He was absolutely terrified, and she had no idea how she missed that the first time. It was etched into every crease and fold of flesh. His chest moved in and out with rapid breathing. His mouth was wide open, and she saw the fillings in his back molars. His voice came out broken, afraid.

Lisa!

How could he know her name? He was unconscious when he came in the first time. Could he still hear as she tried to pump his heart?

Lisa!

She clamped her hands over her ears, but the sound of his voice, screaming, was still there inside her. She stumbled backward into the empty room as the stretcher, guided by the robed figures, turned toward the room. Lisa kept walking until her head bumped into the wall. She watched as the hideous, screaming man was wheeled under the strobing light. The stretcher came into the room, rushing straight at Lisa. She froze and screamed as if she were an animal caught in the headlights of an oncoming car, just as the stench and wailing and metal frame of the bed were about to smash into her body.

She closed her eyes, and the sound vanished, and when Lisa opened her eyes again, the patient, the robed figures, and the stretcher were all gone.

The room was empty.

Of course, it was.

She looked back to Meagan, to Patrick. They were both moving in time now, too, occupied with their tasks.

Machines beeped, monitors flashed with rhythms and blood pressures and statistics. But that didn't make her heart beat any slower. If anything, it made her more afraid.

5

Lisa walked to the staff bathroom as fast as she could, went inside, and locked the door behind her. She let out a breath she didn't even realize she had been holding. Her hands shook as she gripped the edge of the sink and squeezed the porcelain until her knuckles burned.

A hallucination. That's what it was. But she wasn't even high. She reached into her pocket and pulled out the syringe of fentanyl. It was still full.

Vivid, dreamlike images brought on by stress, that had to be it. Her mind projected visual representations of her fears, using what she had seen recently as a warning. She took a deep breath in, then let it out slowly. She closed her eyes tight.

The call with the lawyer had caught her off guard. Her marriage was beyond repair, and she was terrified of losing Sean. Then, to see a patient like that, well, it was just too much. Something cracked. Something in her mind.

Lisa didn't want to look at herself in the mirror. Didn't want to see those small, sharp teeth again. But she forced herself to meet her gaze, to stare into her own eyes. She waited for the reflection to move, to smile, to do something the real Lisa standing in the bathroom wasn't doing. The longer she stared at herself, the less like her it seemed. Her eyes, nose, mouth, hair…all of it, Lisa Morton, but those features looked so sad, so lost. Her skin was pale, blotchy. Bruise-colored half-circles sagged under her eyes, eyes coursed with bright red veins. There were lines around her mouth she'd never seen before, lines that only appeared when she was trying not to cry. Maybe she wasn't faking being okay as well as she thought she'd been. Maybe everyone could see the turmoil inside her, the struggle, the failure.

Her thoughts moved, were pulled inward. It was a feeling she knew all too well. That black hole in her head was unfolding, spreading. It gripped the edge of every bright thought, every piece of hope, of happiness, and vacuumed it to the center of itself, shredding it all in the process, leaving nothing but the dark, the heavy, the depressing.

She felt the black hole, just like she did the day Mark asked her to name the good things in her life. Only now there was no Mark. And from inside that black hole (she could almost see it as much as she felt it, a pitch-black circle in the middle of her brain) came a low voice. It was not her voice. At least she didn't think it was. It spoke in sibilant whispers that reminded her of how a snake would talk if it had language.

It's not right for you to feel this much pain. It said.

Lisa lowered her head to avoid her eyes. "It's just living. Everyone feels this way sometimes."

True. And everyone does what they must to avoid being buried beneath it. You feel buried, don't you, Lisa?

"Every day. All the time."

Take the pain away, just for a little while.

"I can't."

But you can. You have it right there in your pocket.

Lisa's hand reached into the pocket of her scrub jacket, and her fingers felt the hard plastic of the syringe. Such a small amount of liquid, and yet…what it contained was endless.

She shook her head. "No. I have to be better for Sean. I have to be strong."

Was that a laugh?

Strong? You think suffering through every single day is strength? You think obsessing over every mistake you've ever made is changing anything? Be strong tomorrow. Tonight, you need to take away the pain. Make it stop hurting.

"Not anymore," Lisa said. "Maybe the way I feel is what I deserve. Maybe this is exactly how I *should* feel."

Why did you take the syringe, then? If you never meant to erase the hurt, why steal the medicine?

Because I fail, Lisa thought. That's what I do. I am good intentions and poor decisions.

No change ever happened in a day. Take small steps, the voice said. *You can't move forward if you hurt all the time. Give yourself a break every once in a while. Look at yourself. The pain is written all over your face.*

She looked, and she wished she hadn't. The voice was right. It was all there. She wasn't fooling anybody. The black hole kept sucking in the light, uncovering the thoughts and feelings she tried so hard to keep hidden.

Worthless.

Failure.

Selfish.

Bad mother.

Bad wife.

No future.

The list went on and on, and it was all she could see.

Just a little. Just for tonight. Tomorrow will be better, and you'll be stronger.

"No, not tomorrow. Right now."

It's too much right now. And you know that. It's too much for you to carry by yourself. Ease the burden. You deserve some peace. It hurt so much, Lisa. Doesn't it? It's killing you, the constant, unending pain. Isn't it?

She still had one hand in her pocket. The other hand moved to her head, gripped her skull. How could that small mass of flesh hidden under all that hair and bone cause her so much trouble?

Isn't it? The voice said again.

"Yes."

Just a little bit, Lisa. Just a little to get you through right now. Every moment decides its own outcome. Think, last week you wouldn't have hesitated. But here you are, talking about being strong for Sean, and all you're doing is suffering. Your body is aching. I know it is. You feel weak and sick. Look at your hands. Look at how they're shaking. You need a little to get by.

Hearing Sean's name made Lisa see her son's face. Not as he was, but as she made him. Injured. The terrified look on his face as her fingers grabbed his shirt, pulled him off balance. The fear in his eyes as he fell backward. His small body crashing into the stairs, then crumpling at the bottom. The way he had cried, then. Sucking in breath, moaning. Looking at his mother like he had no idea who she was.

The pain is too much.

"The pain is too much."

Take it away.

Lisa took the syringe from her pocket, twisted off the top, and put the end to her mouth. She pushed gently, just a little until her tongue was flooded with a bitter taste. She swallowed, went over to the sink and rinsed out her mouth, then popped in a piece of gum.

She felt regret instantly. She wanted to be strong, and this wasn't strength. But it was too late. There was no un-ringing the bell she had rung. The medicine was already slipping through her bloodstream, blunting the edges of all those sharp thoughts the black hole did not want to devour. Her head went light. She closed her eyes and let the feeling overtake her.

6

"Lisa?"

She heard the voice, knew it was her name being called, but it didn't occur to her to acknowledge it. She was busy watching those double doors, waiting for Burn Man to come bursting through again, howling like an animal with something's jaws clenched around its leg, scraping his skin off on the sheets.

"Lisa?"

She turned and saw Meagan looking at her. What did her face say? Hard to tell. Amused? Maybe a little. Concerned? Definitely. The kind of look you give someone when you know they've received bad news.

"You okay?"

"Yeah, fine," Lisa said. "Tired, you know? Long days, long nights."

Meagan nodded. God, her eyelashes were long. Lisa imagined them growing even longer and thicker, like the leaves on some tropical tree, until they were so big they'd make Meagan topple over, and everyone would laugh at the pretty girl with the crazy lashes.

Lisa shook her head, blinked a few times.

Meagan scrunched up her face and held out a syringe. "If you're not busy, would you mind giving room seven this? It's her antibiotic."

Lisa took the syringe and smiled at Meagan, but it didn't feel right. The skin around her mouth was too tight, so tight, in fact, it felt like a hole might tear right through her cheek.

"Seven," Lisa repeated. "Got it."

"Thanks a ton. I'm still charting on the last patient."

Lisa's shoes squeaked on the tiles, so shiny they looked wet, and she couldn't help but think about how much blood, vomit, shit, and tears had been spilled on these floors. Does it ever really come out? All those inside things that somehow find their way out? No matter how much you cleaned, the blood and shit and piss just kept on coming.

She reached the room and knocked twice before opening the door. An elderly man sat in the bed, as much white hair on his head as there was coming out of his ears and nose. His t-shirt may have been white at one time, but now it was covered in stains, a color-coded index of all the things he spilled on it.

"Where's the other nurse?" the man asked. "The pretty one."

Lisa smiled her best "fuck you" smile and said, "She's busy, so I came to give you your meds. I'm Lisa, by the way. The not-so-pretty nurse."

The man's eyes opened a little wider for a moment, then he smiled, and his teeth matched the yellow stains under his arms.

"Oh hon, I didn't mean nothing by it. I just forgot her name, is all. Margaret. Molly. I don't know, something with an M. You're just as pretty, don't you worry. Can't see for shit anyway. Figure if I tell the nurses they're pretty, they might want me to live just a little longer."

The patient laughed, and it was a nice laugh. A voice used to laughing long and hard at things that weren't very funny, and Lisa liked that about him. She liked that trait in just about anyone. See all the shit in the world, all the lies and corruption and pain and heartache, and just laugh at it. Laugh like it's the best fucking joke you've ever heard.

"So what you got there?" the patient asked. "Something to make me young and handsome again?"

Lisa held up the syringe. "You wish. Just something to kill all those bugs that decided to set up camp in your lungs."

"All right. Let's get it over with, so I can go home. Got a dog that gets all depressed if I'm gone for too long, then he starts shitting on my bed to get revenge. The vet says he's blind, but I just think he's faking."

"What kind of dog?" Lisa asked as she took the cap off the syringe and twisted it onto the man's IV.

"Don't know. Little bit of everything, I guess. Everything and nothing. He's worthless pretty much except for petting when you feel down. Ever pet a dog when you're in the dumps? Perks you right up."

With the syringe locked, Lisa started pushing the plunger. The cloudy white liquid moved slowly into the IV.

"This will feel a little cold," she said.

"Lisa!"

There it was again, a voice calling her name. Lisa stopped pushing the medicine and listened. What would come first, the smell of burning or the stretcher through the doors? For how long would the ghost of Burn Man keep repeating his last moments over and over again?

"Lisa, stop!"

Meagan came running into the room, one arm straight in front of her, reaching. Even with all that makeup on, her skin had gone pale. That outreached hand swatted at Lisa's hand, the one holding the syringe. It was a hard swat, and even through the glove, it hurt.

Lisa backed away. "What is the matter with you?"

Meagan, out of breath, untwisted the syringe from the IV.

"Oh my god," she said. "Oh my god. Sir, I'm so sorry."

She reached into her pocket for a saline syringe, shot the liquid into the trash can near her feet, then connected it and pulled fluid out of the man's IV until blood entered the tubing.

"What the hell is going on?" the patient asked.

Was it Lisa's imagination, or was the room tilting a bit? Slowly turning like the hands on a clock?

Meagan turned to Lisa, her eyes big and afraid.

"Seven," she said. "Room seven."

"I know," Lisa said. "Room seven, give the antibiotic."

Meagan shook her head. "This is room six, Lisa. This patient has a severe allergy to antibiotics." She took a few deep breaths, said, "Oh my god," a few more times under her breath.

The patient lifted his arm, looked at the IV, then up at Lisa. His face darkened, and his lips tightened.

"You didn't double-check anything, did you?" the man said. "Just came in here and started giving meds all willy nilly."

There went her heart again, beating too fast, too hard. The room tilted just a little further, and she put a hand on the sink. Heat flushed on the back of her neck, crawled up her scalp.

Lisa said. "I made a mistake."

"God damn right you did. Holy shit, lady."

The patient turned his arm as if he might see a rash, or hives, blossoming on his skin. He looked to Meagan. "I want to speak with a manager or charge nurse. Someone. I'm not okay with this one bit." He looked at Lisa. "Check my god damn chart, look at the medical alert bracelet I wear. Look at my name band. Something, anything. You fucked up, lady. Big time."

"I know," Lisa tried to say, but the words just came out as a small moan. She was going to fall over if everything didn't stop moving. Gravity would pull her across the room, throw her into the other wall. And her head, it was somewhere far above her body. Disconnected and floating.

"I'm so sorry. I've had a…" Lisa reached for the patient's IV to disconnect the syringe, but the man yanked his arm away. His eyes flashed wide, then narrowed. His voice dropped to a low growl.

"You're not touching me." He nodded toward Meagan. "She can do it. I want you out right now."

Meagan wouldn't even look at Lisa. She brushed past her and unscrewed the syringe. Lisa inched her away to the door. She stared at the man in the bed, and for one brief moment, she saw him as he would have been—had she given the antibiotic. She saw his eyes grow so big they seemed to protrude from their sockets. She saw his hands reach for his throat, which she knew without knowing, was swelling shut. The man's skin tone changed color, grew gray and ashen, his lips as blue as Sean's tongue after eating raspberry jelly beans.

All because of her.

"I'm really sorry," Lisa said as she backed away.

The man looked straight at her, and she saw the anger in his eyes.

"When you stop caring," he said, "that's when you start fucking up. Get it together or get a new job."

"It's been a hard day," Lisa said, and her voice sounded weak.

"Leave your personal shit outside," the patient said. "You think I give a fuck how hard your day was? Then don't come to work if you can't handle it. I trust you to do your job no matter what kind of shit you've got going on."

Lisa opened her mouth to apologize again, but what was the point? The patient was right. She fucked up.

7

Outside the room, she stood with her back to the wall. She looked up at the fluorescent lights until her eyes burned and sun spots moved across her vision. She felt absolutely awful. Guilty, yes, but even more than that, she felt physically sick. And it was more than just her mistake. Somehow, that error already seemed far away, receding into a foggy distance. Here, outside the room, her thoughts were swift, electric things that sparked like eels in a black sea.

Shoes tapped on the tile floor, coming closer. Someone stood behind Lisa, and she turned around to see who it was, but her eyes were still filled with bursting light-flowers, and all she saw was a dark shape.

She blinked until her eyes watered. A voice spoke.

"Lisa, we need to talk."

"Charlotte?" Lisa said.

"Come with me, please."

The dark shape moved down the hall, and Lisa followed, keeping one hand against the wall to guide her. The farther they walked, the more Lisa's eyes cleared up, and she saw Charlotte walking quickly toward her office.

Once inside, Charlotte did not ask Lisa to sit. She crossed her arms over her chest and looked directly into Lisa's eyes. Lisa noticed the faint smell of perfume, even though it was a rule of Charlotte's that the nurses not wear anything scented while on the job.

Hypocrite, Lisa thought.

"I'm going to ask you a question, and I'm only going to ask once," Charlotte said. The lines in her forehead deepened. She was not much older than Lisa, but she had something that the administration recognized as necessary for leading an Emergency Department. A special something...what was it? Oh yes. Bitchiness. A don't-fuck-with-me attitude and a preference for micro-managing that made life miserable for everyone.

"Okay," Lisa said.

Charlotte was tall and too thin. She probably thought it was the right amount, but it wasn't. Lisa recognized obsessiveness, and she knew without a doubt that Charlotte was counting every calorie, then sweating all of them out on a treadmill every night. As a result, she looked unhealthy, maybe even sick, and her face was gaunt. Her too-blue eyes stared out from deep sockets.

"What did you do with the fentanyl that you checked out for the patient who expired?" Charlotte asked.

Because of Charlotte's height, Lisa had to tilt her head to look at her, and it made her feel like she was back in school, in the principal's office, being asked to explain why she grabbed Ali Sanders's ponytail and tried to rip it off. Lisa had to fight back a laugh.

"I threw it away," Lisa said.

"Where?"

"In the…uh…in the bin. The medication disposal bin."

Charlotte shifted her weight from one leg to the other. She moved one hand to her hip. Her legs looked like something Lisa could easily break if she wanted to.

"I looked," Charlotte said. "I didn't see any fentanyl syringes."

"Well, maybe I accidentally threw it in the trash. I don't know. It was stressful, a little chaotic."

Charlotte leaned in. "You haven't been acting the same since that patient died."

"Death will do that," Lisa said.

"That's not what I mean, and you know it."

"I really don't know what you mean."

Charlotte straightened up. "Several of your co-workers feel you aren't acting in control of yourself, and it seems that you are not even aware of it. A full syringe of fentanyl is missing, and you are now acting under the influence."

"I—" Lisa started.

Charlotte held up a hand. "I'm not finished. I've asked security to call you a cab. You are to be placed on leave effective immediately while this situation is under investigation. You are also to submit a urine sample before you leave."

Lisa let her gaze drift to the floor, to the awful greyish-purple carpet in Charlotte's office. Why they would put carpet anywhere in a hospital, Lisa could never understand.

So, this was it. Her nursing license would be gone

within weeks. She'd have no job, no husband, no son. She had always wondered how people find themselves with a life that's no longer worth living, and the answer saddened her. It happened fast. Faster than she ever thought it could.

"I'm sorry," Lisa said quietly.

"Are you admitting guilt?" Charlotte asked.

"No, I'm just sorry for everything."

Charlotte nodded slowly but didn't say anything.

Through the window in the door, Lisa could see two security guards standing just outside. Waiting. She could also see her backpack hanging on the coat rack near the nurse's station. Her car keys were inside. If she could just reach that…

"Unless you have anything else to say, it's time to go," Charlotte said.

Lisa took a deep breath, closed her eyes. She opened her mouth like she was going to speak, then spun around and threw open the door. It crashed into the wall, startling the security guards, and Lisa took off running down the hallway. The squeak of her shoes was trumpet-loud, playing an off-time tune as she ran. Her top half felt heavy, but her legs felt bird-bone light.

She struggled to keep from toppling over as the

room did a little tick-tock tumble to the right. Her blue backpack was just up ahead. She heard voices shouting her name, another voice shouting "ma'am," and for a second, she wondered if someone else was on the run.

Then she realized she was the "ma'am." She smiled at that as her shoes squeaked.

Patrick stood up from his station, the shoe website still open on his screen, and stared with big eyes as Lisa ran by. She barely slowed down to grab her backpack off the hook, and those same double-doors the Burn Man had come through opened up on a motion sensor, and within seconds Lisa was out in the cold, open-air, sucking up the dark night into her lungs and breathing out steam.

8

Lisa drove. Her mind felt simultaneously numb and alert, the steering wheel a too-big circle in her too-small hands. She drove cautiously down east Portland streets, half expecting the flashing lights and siren of a cop car to come screaming after her.

Would they send the cops?

Lisa honestly didn't know. She'd never been in this situation, and she hadn't heard of anyone being confronted about drug use on the job. Still, she wouldn't go home. Not right away, in case they were waiting for her.

She slowly took one hand off the wheel and reached into the pocket of her scrubs. Her fingers searched until she found the syringe of medicine. She pumped the brake for a hard stop at a red light, then dripped a couple of drops under her tongue, closed her eyes, and still saw the red light shining through her eyelids.

She thought of Sean, of all the times she told him about how people sometimes put things in their bodies to take away pain, but it can make them clumsy and stupid, and sometimes...sometimes they even accidentally kill people when they drive while feeling that way.

Hypocrite! Liar! Fraud!

There's a hole in my head, she thought. *A hole right in the skull, and when it rains, the water gets in short circuits everything.*

The light she saw through her closed eyes turned green. She pushed the gas and was halfway through the intersection before her opened her eyes again. She turned down one street, then another, glancing between the windshield and the rearview mirror.

Rearview.

To see all that's behind you. She smiled a sloppy smile and felt something wet drip from her chin. She wiped away the drool and kept on driving.

She saw a stop sign only after she'd passed it. She rolled down the window and hoped the cold air would do something for her heavy arms, her burning eyes.

Lisa had no idea where she was. Maybe in daylight, she would have recognized it, but not at night, not in this state.

Something rattled under the hood of the car. The awful sound of metal parts clanking together. She pushed the gas pedal down harder, and the engine went to work, but the car didn't move any faster. Those metal sounds came again, and then the engine sputtered and died. Lisa did her best to steer off the road. One tire jumped the curb, and the car rolled to a stop.

Why not? The perfect end to a day where everything falls apart. This is how it had to end, right? Like she was ever going to make it back home and sleep this one off. Some days just careened into chaos, dismantling all the fragile pieces of our lives until we slip off to dreamland in the glass shards of whatever person we believed ourselves to be.

Lisa wanted to cry, but she couldn't. Whatever wires would have allowed it were disconnected or frayed. Probably the fentanyl.

She grabbed her backpack and got out of the car, shivered in the cold. She looked down at her feet and saw a black circle on the road. Darker than the asphalt around it, slick too. Roadwork, maybe. Smoother asphalt than all the other stuff.

She stepped up onto the sidewalk. Just a normal neighborhood, like any other. Old Portland, old houses, most with their lights out. Except for the one she'd stopped in front of. Hard to tell in just the moonlight, but it looked gray or something close to it. A rundown two-story house with a sagging front porch. The tree in the yard looked dead. Bare branches, trunk split down the middle. Lightning, probably.

The house was completely dark, and the two windows in the second story were covered with black curtains, which made them look like dead eyes and the front door a mouth. There was no breeze at all, but the curtains in one window fluttered with movement as if someone were pressed against them and walking back and forth.

Lisa squinted, shook her head. A body shape appeared in the curtain fabric, and Lisa gasped, took a step backward.

Her engine trouble must have awakened someone inside. Maybe they were looking down to see what was going on.

Lisa was about to move, to walk until she found a bar or a gas station, and figure out exactly where she was and how far it was to home, when the front door of the gray house creaked open. A soft, red light came from inside. Red like the light when Lisa held a flashlight to her hand and showed Sean how all the blood inside was illuminated.

"Just under your skin," she'd told him. "Blood, moving everywhere, giving your organs, your muscles, your skin what it needs to be healthy."

And what had she done? What had she put in her blood?

The red light stretched onto the front porch and into the yard. There was something inviting about it. Welcoming.

Lisa took the walkway to the porch, went up the unlevel steps, and stopped at the open door. The living room just inside was completely bare. No carpet, no rugs, no furniture, and no person. The whole room was bathed in that red light. Where was it coming from? Lisa couldn't see any source? There were no lamps, no bulbs glowing from the ceiling. Just a light that seemed to come from everywhere. From nowhere.

It made Lisa think of what her grandmother used

to say about an unkept house in her neighborhood: "It's a place you want to enter softly and tiptoe out of when you leave."

Lisa took one step inside, suddenly wanting to find the source of the red light, to understand how it could make light such a color.

"I'm Lisa Morton," she said out loud. "My stupid car broke down, and I'm trying to figure out where I am. Think I got a little turned around."

She felt strange walking into the house, but obviously someone had seen her and opened the door to welcome her in. Someone who wanted to help.

Some alarm bells went off in her head, but they were soft and distant. Memories of news stories about missing and dead women who had made stupid mistakes in their last moments alive. Mistakes like walking into houses that looked a lot like this.

What the hell did she care? What could someone take from her that the world hadn't already stolen?

In the center of the living room was a small, round table with objects on it, but she couldn't see what they were. She walked closer, and her footsteps echoed deep into the house. The walls were stained with black mold that grew in shadow patterns, and the wood floor beneath her feet was deeply scarred.

She turned around, and the front door was closed. She had not heard it, and there was no breeze to make it shut on its own.

Her heart tripped a few times, like a marching soldier stumbling over his boots.

"I don't know anything about cars," Lisa said. "I'd be really grateful if you could take a look, tell me what you think is wrong."

She walked closer to the small table and saw a glass of water. The liquid inside was pinkish from the red light, and it made her think of blood pulled up through an IV. In a line next to the glass were nine small pills and a handwritten note. Pills, all different sizes and colors— pink, blue, and red. The note, written in a scribble, was still legible.

It said, "Failure."

Lisa choked at how fast the tears came.

She understood. Somehow, Mark, her ex-husband, had planned all this. Who else could have done it? Who else knew how she saw herself, her problems? It was that bastard, tempting her using the one thing he knew she could not turn away from.

She would show him. What's the worst that could happen? She'd fall asleep and never wake up. She'd hit the floor, foam bubbling out of her mouth, and slip into unconsciousness while the universe opened its arms and welcomed her home.

That's the best you got, Mark?

Some part of her, the angel on one shoulder, maybe, tried to convince her she was something more than that one word written on the note. But she no longer saw herself. She looked inward and didn't see a person. She forgot her name. When she tried to think of it, to find it in her mind, all she saw was the word "Failure."

Lisa knelt by the table in the red light, picked up the pills, and put them in her mouth. The bitter taste on her tongue was a comfort. Bitter first, sweet later. She grabbed the glass and drank half of it down. The liquid inside burned her eyes, then her mouth, her throat.

Then she wept, and she waited.

9

Henry Thayer sat in his favorite chair by the window, smoking a cigarette. He had watched the woman's car sputter and stop. Had watched the door of that terrible house open and welcome her. And like a fool, she'd gone inside.

Thayer smoked and watched, hoping, praying that she would come back out. When the clock on the mantle said, 2 A.M., Thayer stubbed out his cigarette, got up, and went outside.

He paused at the two black circles in the street. One a father, the other a son. One made it. The other did not. His old knees popped as he walked up the porch steps. He hissed at the pain and kept going until he reached the front door.

Thayer didn't knock. He knew it would be open. It always was. And the house was always empty. The cops had searched it how many times? And every time, it was the same.

Nothing there, no evidence of drugs or anything illegal. And as far as the house itself? Apparently, it was owned and not by a bank, so there was nothing to repossess.

Thayer put his hand on the door knob, half-expecting it to send an electric shock through his body and stop his heart. But the knob turned, and the door creaked open.

The house was completely dark. Thayer stepped inside, said, "Miss? Miss, my name is Henry Thayer. I just wanted to see if you were all right."

He stood still for a few seconds, listening and letting his eyes adjust. He started to see the vague shapes of walls, a staircase, but nothing else.

He took his cellphone from his pocket, turned on the flashlight, and moved the beam over the floor. The light illuminated a black shoe, attached to a leg wearing blue pants, scrub pants it looked like. Thayer moved the light until he saw her body lying motionless in the empty room. Nothing else around her. No furniture, no pills, no liquor bottles, no syringes or pipes. Just a body.

Thayer rushed over and fell to his knees, grabbed the woman's shoulders, and shook her gently. From the moment his hand touched her, Thayer knew she was gone. There was something not alive in the feel of her, the stiffness, maybe. The lack of warmth. The silence of a person not breathing.

Thayer whispered, "God damn it."

His eyes filled with tears, and he hated that he felt responsible for things that were not his fault.

"I could have helped," he said to the dead woman. "Whatever it was, you would have made it through."

Thayer lifted the cellphone, dialed 911, and told the operator he needed an ambulance.

10

Thayer stood just outside the gray house, watching as the cop cars and the ambulance drove away. None of the vehicles used their lights, which was just about the saddest thing Thayer could think of. *Hopeless,* they seemed to say. Not even worth flashing lights and sirens. Already gone, already lost.

God, how he hated that house. He stretched his neck and looked up at the dilapidated property. It seemed to breathe at him, to expand and contract, to move against the sky as if preparing to open its door-mouth and swallow him.

For Henry Thayer, he had seen the last life come to ruin because of this place. He believed—right or wrong, it didn't matter—that God had placed him here for such a time as this. Where others might turn a blind eye and ignore what was happening, Thayer would do something. He had to.

It made him angry that the pull of the house even seemed to affect him. He hadn't smoked in how long, and now he was sucking the cancer sticks every night—oh, what Alice would say if she could see him now.

Thayer shivered, put his hands in his pocket, and crossed the street back to his place.

He opened up the garage door and went over to the lawn mower. Once again, he shined his cellphone flashlight until he found what he was looking for. A small, red gas can he used to fill the mower and weed whacker.

He picked it up, patted his sweater pocket, and nodded when he felt what was in there.

He said a quick prayer as he went back across the street, walking with determined steps. He marched straight up the porch stairs, threw open the front door, and went into the empty living room.

He felt, somehow, that he could still sense a presence in the house. Not something evil, but the woman who had died. As if her spirit was still in there, wandering. Probably just in his head, but he felt it all the same.

Thayer thought of his friend Zach Ayers, the young man who had survived a fiery ride to hell. He thought of Zach's dad, who had burned to death just outside after riding the same bike. All tricks of the same trickster.

Thayer unscrewed the cap from the gas can, lifted it, and poured the liquid out onto the floor. The fumes burned his nostrils as he went around the room, splashing the gas all over the walls.

"If it's fire you want, it's fire you'll get," Thayer said, and air moved through the house, blowing from upstairs and pushing past Thayer as it rushed out the front door. A long exhale.

Thayer closed his eyes then reached into his sweater pocket for the cigarette lighter. His thumb glides over the rough surface of the flint, feeling the ridges along his skin. He flicks it once, and it only sparks. Then, slowly, all around him, a red light grows. Faint at first, it gets brighter, as if on a dimmer switch until the room is filled with a red glow. Thayer feels like he's inside the mouth of a beast, a dragon, and the fire in its belly is getting ready to devour a new victim.

He turned around, and where there was once

nothing, there was now a table in the center of the room. Just a table and a lamp. The bulb inside glowed red, but it was not the light source that pulsed on the walls, the ceiling.

Sweat ran down his neck as he looked at that table, at what was on it. The only secret he ever had in his life, lying there in plain sight. Waiting for him, inviting him. It had been years, but still, he felt a pull, like some deep part of himself had always wanted it again. He knew he couldn't, he promised he wouldn't, and so far, he had kept that promise.

How could the house know? No one knew. No one except Alice, and she was gone. His fingers tightened into a fist. His nails scratched the palm of his hand, and the sweat kept crawling down his back. He tried to flick the lighter again, and it was still just a blue spark.

He approached the table and tapped one of the legs with his foot—just to know it was real. It was. Which meant the thing on the table was probably real as well. Thayer became aware of his heartbeat, the lub-dub sound of it pumping blood through his body. He heard it, felt it behind his eyes. His hand opened and closed.

He hated what was on the table, and he hated himself for ever loving it. Destroyer of relationships.

Scorcher of trust. Vile, disgusting, shameful. And now he hated that he wanted it again. He never would have sought it out, never would have gone searching. He had worked so hard to repair the damage it had done to his life, his marriage. Alice forgave him, but she never forgot. Who could? Even years later, after he had gotten better, he would see his beloved wife stare off in a trance as if looking into the past and remembering what her husband was capable of, and her eyes would fill with sadness. And Thayer knew, without her ever saying a word, that he was the reason for that sadness. His desires, urges, needs. His lack of self-control and his lies to keep it in the dark.

Now here it was. Pulsing with red light, and his heart pulsed in time with the shadows on the walls. He wiped sweat from his eyes and walked a little closer. He wanted it so badly. He'd forgotten how bad he could want something.

Henry Thayer looked at the cigarette lighter in his hand, then at the table. He closed his eyes, said a prayer, and made his choice.

About the Author

Tyler Jones is the author of *Criterium*, *The Dark Side of the Room*, *Enter Softly*, and *Almost Ruth*. His work has appeared in the anthologies *Midnight from Beyond the Stars*, *Flame Tree Press: Chilling Crime Short Stories*, *Campfire Macabre*, *Paranormal Contact*, *Burnt Tongues*, *One Thing Was Certain*, *101 Proof Horror*, and in *Dark Moon Digest*, *Coffin Bell*, *Cemetery Dance*, *LitReactor*, *Aphotic Realm*, and *The NoSleep Podcast*.

His stories have been optioned for film.

He lives in Portland, Oregon.

www.tylerjones.net
Twitter: @tjoneswriter
Instagram: @tjoneswriter

THE DARK SIDE OF THE ROOM

TYLER JONES

AUTHOR OF CRITERIUM

THE DARK SIDE OF THE ROOM
Extended Edition

**Includes an introduction by
Philip Fracassi (*Beneath a Pale Sky*)
and the novella *Along the Shadow***

Available in paperback, hardcover, and ebook

"Genuinely unsettling and leaking of paranoid dread, *The Dark Side of the Room* is residential horror at its finest."
**—Max Booth III,
author of *We Need to Do Something***

"What struck me the hardest was the delicate beauty of the telling. There's a tight-wired fragility to the prose, to the story, that creates a sense of both awe and uncertainty. A grisly tale, an ever-so-slow twisting of a knife. A triumphant piece of fiction."
**—Philip Fracassi, author of
Beneath a Pale Sky and *Behold the Void***

ALMOST RUTH

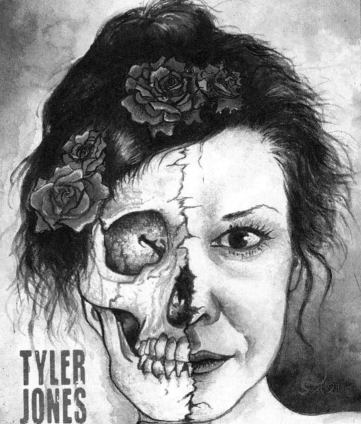

TYLER
JONES

ALMOST RUTH

Available in paperback, hardcover, and ebook

Ashville is a town with a secret history. Ancient structures lie hidden in the woods, and strange rituals are performed to keep the dead where they belong. For gravedigger Abel Cunningham, it is also a town filled with regrets. And when Abel is tasked with an unusual burial, he discovers there are more than just corpses in the cemetery.

Set in an unsettling vision of the Old West, **Almost Ruth** is the new nightmare from the author of **Criterium** and **The Dark Side of the Room**

"Tyler Jones writes with the lyrical complexity and haunting tenderness of masters like Matheson and Straub while remaining entirely new and inventive. A true visionary of contemporary horror fiction."
—**Eric LaRocca, author of *Things Have Gotten Worse Since We Last Spoke***

"Tyler Jones shows us in *Almost Ruth* that he is a fierce talent in the horror genre and one not to be missed, with prose as sharp as a scalpel he cuts us wide open and pours salt into our wounds.
—**Ross Jeffery, Bram Stoker Nominated author of *Tome, Juniper,* and *Only The Stains Remain***

"With unmatched depth and painstaking beauty, Jones crafts a story focused on small town rituals reminiscent of Shirley Jackson. One that will keep your gears turning and your blood chilled long after the last page."
—**Brennan LaFaro, author of *Slattery Falls***

ENTER SOFTLY

Available in paperback, hardcover, and ebook

Enter Softly collects the brand new novellas that are included in the extended editions of *Criterium*, *The Dark Side of the Room*, and the new novel *Almost Ruth*.

In *Along the Shadow*, a story from the world of *The Dark Side of the Room*, Detective Gary Shaw is called to the scene of an unusual and grisly murder, which leads him to chase after a strange suspect. But Shaw is not sure if the suspect is also chasing him'.

The butler for a wealthy family begins to fear the worst when mysterious guests show up at the manor in *Wake Up*, a prequel story to the novel *Almost Ruth*.

And in *Enter Softly*, Emergency Room nurse, Lisa Morton, has a problem and she is about to lose her marriage, her child, and her job. As she works the night shift a very damaged patient comes into the hospital and sets in motion a series of events that could lead to Lisa's salvation, or her end. A companion novella to the critically acclaimed *Criterium*, Tyler Jones returns to a world where addiction is a force with teeth and claws, and it will not let you go quietly.

BURN THE PLANS

coming 2022 from Cemetery Gates Media

From Tyler Jones (author of *Criterium*, *The Dark Side of the Room*, and *Almost Ruth*) comes *Burn the Plans*, a collection featuring fourteen tales of supernatural suspense.

In "A Sharp Black Line", children go missing whenever a ghostly island appears in the center of a river during a storm, and a father must make a terrible choice.

Two young brothers are tasked with burying the family dog, and uncover dark family secrets in "Trigger."

In "Red Hands", a disturbed man goes on a killing spree, and his childhood friend suspects it has something to do with what they found, many years ago, hidden in a cave.

A courtroom sketch artist draws the evil she cannot see in "The Devil on the Stand."

A young boy sets out to get photographic proof of the ghosts that haunt his home in "Boo!"

Grotesque government experiments, a remote viewer who blurs past and future, a crate that contains ancient evil, and bloodthirsty machines are all part of the world in which these tales take place.

Featuring thirteen short stories and one novelette, Burn the Plans is a relentless journey into the dark places we end up when all of our plans go wrong.

Made in the USA
Columbia, SC
28 December 2021

52876350R00162